A Different Alchemy

This is a work of fiction. Names, characters, places, and incidents are the products of the author's imagination or are used fictitiously. Any resemblance to actual events, locales, or persons, living or dead, is coincidence.

Published in the United States by CreateSpace Independent Publishing.

ISBN-13: 978-1493792160

ISBN-10: 1493792164

Cover Design: Truenotdreams Design

Author Photo: Jodie McFadden

ALSO BY CHRIS DIETZEL

Apocalyptic
The Man Who Watched The World End
The Hauntings of Playing God
The Last Teacher

Dystopian
The Theta Timeline
The Theta Prophecy
The Theta Patient

A Different Alchemy

Chris Dietzel

"It set him free," said Lee. "It gave him the right to be a man, separate from every other man."

"That's lonely."

"All great and precious things are lonely."

- John Steinbeck

- East of Eden

Chapter 1

A stream of black clouds swirled skyward from the stadium, hovering above it like the stormy portal to another world. The smoke was so great, so immense, that even from miles away Jeffrey expected to be able to hear the roar of flames. Instead, it was eerily quiet; the silence of being within the eye of a hurricane, the visible proof of destruction that came from being outside it. Not even the traffic, swarming all around him, seemed to make noise at that moment.

It was as if the entire world had gone silent.

The quiet was interrupted by his car radio. The staticky voice said the fire had quickly grown out of control until the blaze could be seen arcing over the top row of seats. Expecting to see flames spitting into the air, Jeffrey looked toward the stadium. All he could see, though, was the smoke.

"There are thousands of people gathered around the stadium," the voice said. "It looks like some of the people were having another Block protest and others were celebrating the upcoming relocation to Washington. Some people are still holding up protest signs. Others are drinking beer and cheering."

Protesting the Blocks was nothing new. From the moment it became clear that the only children who could be born would look just like other kids, but would be motionless, quiet, and unable to have children of their own, there were parts of society that resented having to accommodate the silent masses. This rally, though, had seemed different even before the fire started.

It had only taken Jeffrey a minute to leave the base and get back out to the main road. Once on the freeway, however, traffic had immediately slowed.

The voice came from the radio: "The fire is out of control now! There were thousands of Blocks in that stadium."

Dear God, Jeffrey thought, *please don't let my boy be in there*.

He dialed Katherine at home. The phone kept ringing until it finally went to the answering machine. He tried her cell phone. That also rang and rang. He called home again, then her cell again.

The entire time he couldn't help but stare at the giant cloud of smoke. Everyone in the cars around him stared at it too. He turned the volume back up on the radio in the hope that the background noise would let him stop worrying about his wife and son. But everything the man said only made things worse: "The stadium was filled with thousands of Blocks… I don't know what's happening… the fire is everywhere now… oh my God… there's fire everywhere."

There was nothing but silence then, and Jeffrey wondered if the helicopter hadn't landed to try and help save at least a few of the motionless bodies. Helicopter pilots had become a rare commodity. It was possible the helicopter had crashed into the ground at the hands of a rookie pilot. To his disappointment, the man's voice came back on the air a minute later, saying the chopper was moving further away from the stadium because the smoke and fumes were overwhelming. The sound of the helicopter flicked in and out between the man's words to make it seem like a war must be going on and gunfire would soon breakout.

A woman in the car next to him cried hysterically while she stared at the fire. Her eyes closed then and her hands tore at her scalp. Strands of dark hair covered her fists. Her car, only barely moving because of the traffic, drifted slowly toward the guardrail until sparks began to fly. Even as the car scraped, metal against metal, she screamed and cried, all the while flecks of beautiful light flying in every direction. She was still sobbing, eyes still closed, as Jeffrey's car distanced itself from hers. It wasn't difficult to imagine what she must be thinking: *If I can only close my eyes hard enough I can wake from this awful nightmare... Why aren't I waking up?*

He tried Katherine's cell phone again and again. Each time, it rang until her recorded voice came on.

"There's no reason for something like this to happen," the man on the radio said. "No reason. How could someone do this? They weren't hurting anyone."

A driver to Jeffrey's left was screaming as he repeatedly punched the steering wheel. Finally, the man swerved his car off the road and accelerated as fast as he could. The embankment must have been steeper than the driver thought because the car disappeared from sight and did not return.

He tried Katherine again. Once more, there was no answer.

The sound came back on the radio in mid-yell: "Everything is on fire! The entire stadium is on fire! Everyone outside is leaving the area. The police are just walking away. The entire stadium is burning to the ground."

He turned the radio off. At that moment it seemed like a decent idea to rip the god damn thing out of the console and throw it out the window so it broke into tiny bits and pieces.

Lord knows, he had enough time; it wouldn't slow him down at all. The road was four lanes wide in both directions. Eight lanes of highway designed to get people wherever they needed to go. Ordinarily, that would be plenty of space for the remaining population. But two of the lanes were blocked with abandoned cars left by those who had already decided to head south. The vagrant cars weren't parked in empty mall parking lots. Of course they weren't. They were ditched in the same spot where they got flat tires on the rough roads. Without the city's transportation workers, the cars simply sat there, a haven for birds and whatever else found them. Every once in a while a group of volunteers would spend a Saturday bulldozing discarded automobiles off to either side of the road. The work was futile: a month later the lanes would once again be clogged with a makeshift junkyard.

Now, the two open lanes were blocked by drivers staring at the smoke. The woman who had been driving next to Jeffrey, crying hysterically, was now five car-lengths behind him, still dragging against the guardrail without any thought to where she was going or what she was doing. Probably, she had a son or daughter in that fire. Maybe everyone she loved was being burned alive.

Jeffrey blared his horn, but the driver in front of him could only raise his hands in the air and shrug. A line of cars was ahead of them, all avoiding abandoned vehicles, all swerving around giant potholes randomly scattered across the highway. Hitting just one would mean a lost tire, maybe a lost wheel or axle. And then the traffic jam would become a parking lot.

It wasn't until his car drifted over the next hill, still fifteen miles outside the city, that the extent of the horror could be appreciated. The smoke was black and thick. It had spread across the sky as if sent from an angry god intent on drowning the masses in death. Through it, flames spat out from the sides of the stadium walls. The championship flags lining its top perimeter were replaced by a dark fog. The stadium resembled an outrageously large, albeit stubby, Bunsen burner. On a normal summer's day, the field was said to be twenty or thirty degrees hotter than the actual temperature in the parks and streets. He couldn't imagine how hot the field must be now. Already, the giant scoreboards were probably nothing more than a pile of liquid metal and plastic, the seats melting into the concrete. The motionless bodies that had filled each seat would become sets of charred bones and teeth mixed amongst the boiling plastic.

Please, please don't let Galen be in there.

Each time there was a gap of abandoned cars, the vehicles heading back into the city would break away from their single-file lines and race ahead of each other for a couple of seconds. But each time they had to re-form into a single line, the entire mass of cars was forced to slow down to a crawl, even slower than they had been going before, as each car forced its way back into formation. Horns were blaring. People were yelling at each other.

No one wanted to let other cars back in line. Some of the drivers, realizing their vehicle was one of hundreds available to them on the road—they could get out anytime they wanted and hop into an abandoned sedan or hatchback on the side of the highway—began playing bumper cars with the other drivers. When a car wasn't going fast enough, another driver nudged it forward with his SUV. There would be no insurance claim to file, no police report to fill out. The insurance companies had closed shortly before the banks. The police stations were still open, but they no longer bothered themselves with traffic accidents.

When a car wasn't allowed back in the line of traffic after having raced ahead, it took the bumper off another car and forced its way in. Further up the road, a car sideswiped a minivan, forced it off the road, and took its spot in the line.

As Jeffrey's car finally reached 295, the stadium came into sight once more. What he saw was worse than anything he had ever seen in the military. The stadium was still there where it had always been, but only its outline could be seen anymore. Everything else was smoke or flame. He didn't know fires could be so immense. The sky looked like it might never be blue again. With so much smog in the air, how could it? A miniature sun was sitting in the middle of their city, sending black smoke in the air to blot out the sky as far as anyone could see.

No flashing lights or red trucks gathered around the structure to put the flames out. What could a handful of police or volunteer firemen do against a fire that large? It would be left to burn until the entire thing was gone, as if it had never existed, as though the Blocks inside had never existed, as if one day some men said, "Let's put a pile of rubble and scrap metal in the middle of the city," and that was all that had ever been there. Gone was the stadium in which the Phillies had won the World Series. Gone was the stadium where only the biggest bands stopped by during their world tours.

Please don't let my boy be in there.

Traffic was barely moving at all now. The cars in front of him, just as eager to get back to the city as he was, were all mesmerized by the fireball attached to the ballpark. One man got out of his car to start on foot, but a car behind him, oblivious to the road, ran him over. And still the cars made their way back toward the city.

Jeffrey hesitated as he thought about his next move.

It was important to be sure he was thinking clearly. His car drifted to the shoulder of the road as far as he could get it—the traffic behind him could still continue toward the city—and then started making his way toward the fire by foot. He was walking faster than the cars were driving. He walked past drivers who were screaming or wailing. Only every once in a while did he spot a driver who did not appear distraught but looked completely hypnotized or stunned by what they saw.

Other drivers noticed him walking past their cars and began doing the same thing. One of these people didn't bother to pull his car over before abandoning it and a driver in one of the cars further back got out of his vehicle, chased the man down, and began beating him with his fists, the violence suddenly taking precedence over more rational concerns.

Jeffrey took out his cell phone again. Still walking, he dialed Katherine's number. He was surprised when she answered.

"Where are you?" he asked before she could say anything. "Are you at home?"

"No."

"Where are you?" he said again. "Tell me." When she didn't say anything, he said, "Tell me you aren't near the stadium."

He passed a Mercedes with two flat tires, the old woman behind the wheel still trying to make her car move forward along the busted highway, even though it had given her all it could.

Katherine's silence was the worst part. It made him take heavy breaths, made him grip the phone as tightly as he could so it didn't get away.

“Where are you? Are you at the stadium?” And then, to himself, *Please tell me Galen isn’t there*.

Finally she spoke: “The guy on TV said everyone should bring their Blocks to the stadium. He said there was a humane solution to the problem of getting all of them down to Washington. He said—“ but she stopped talking.

He thought about yelling at her, screaming that he didn’t care what a man on TV said or why she would entrust her son’s safety to him or anyone else that she didn’t know. He thought about yelling, “Where’s Galen?” over and over.

He didn’t, though, because he already knew. The smoke told him exactly where his boy was. His wife not answering her phone told him the same thing. The long line of cars rushing to get back to the city provided yet another confirmation.

Behind him, a car horn started blaring. He couldn’t be sure if Katherine had said something else or not.

“He was my son,” he said above the car horn’s moaning.

“I’m sorry, Jeffrey.”

He stopped walking. His hand fell to his side. Cars were still honking at one another. Two men were fighting in the middle of the highway. A car was in flames, as if jealous of the great fireball miles ahead. A woman ran past him, headed in the direction of the stadium.

“Stop running,” Jeffrey wanted to tell the woman. “There’s nothing left to run to. They’re all dead.” As bad as he felt for the woman, though, he remained silent. She would have to get there and handle the situation however she knew how.

The stadium was still covered in flames. Black

smoke was spreading out so that, from outer space, it must look like the entire east coast was slowly disappearing behind a layer of darkness.

When he put the phone back to his ear, Katherine was saying something, but he didn't hear what it was.

"Please tell me our son wasn't in that stadium."

"Jeffrey, I—"

"Please. Please just tell me he wasn't there, not my boy."

But she didn't say anything and he looked around at the madness filling the highway.

"Did you know this was going to happen?" he asked.

Instead of answering, she began to cry, or was just crying harder so he finally noticed she had been crying the entire time.

"Do you remember when we were young?" she said. "Do you remember that time when—"

He dropped the phone on the road where he stood. Cars were still heading toward the fire, toward his original quest. But he turned and started walking back toward the base. With the road blocked with abandoned vehicles, each car passed him slowly enough that he could see individual drivers. A co-worker, a lieutenant who had, until the Great De-evolution started, been on the fast track for promotion and for becoming a general, passed by him. The two men glanced at each other, but neither man waved or saluted the other.

A woman drove past him as she screamed into her phone. A man drove by, crying so hard he couldn't keep his eyes open, and his car flew off the side of the road where there was no guardrail. None of the other cars slowed to check on him.

Jeffrey thought about the last time he had seen Katherine. It had been that very morning. He remembered what she looked like as she sipped her coffee. He had given her a kiss before walking out the front door and heading to work, the same thing he had done for the past thirty years. For the rest of his life he would have to have that as his final image of her. Better that than to imagine her driving their son to the stadium. Better that than to imagine her dragging Galen out of the car by his arms and leaving him by the stadium entrance. He knew then, each step toward the base slowly taking him away from the burning structure and the city, that he would never see or talk to her again.

Everything he had ever known was taken away from him because of that fire. And with that thought in his mind, he continued walking slowly back toward the base.

Chapter 2

There was a time when things hadn't been so complicated. Even after the Great De-evolution signaled an eventual end to mankind, a sense of normality somehow continued. History had shown that nothing, not even the entire world at war against itself, could make men lose their hope for better days. If the appearance of newborns that couldn't take care of themselves, the last generation, couldn't break people's spirits, it seemed nothing could.

Just as quickly as the scientists said this new disorder affected a hundred percent of the world's population and that a cure was unlikely, people set off to prove them wrong. Every corner of the earth was scoured for a group of people who might not have been affected. Nomadic tribes in the Gobi desert were forced to hand their newborns over for inspection. Eskimos were monitored to see if their environment might have somehow protected them from having Block children. The lone Amazonian tribesman, monitored from the air for years, tormented by curious academics for decades, was hunted down and transported to the nearest laboratory to test his semen. Sadly, the trauma of being bound and dragged away by men driving powered gods overwhelmed the native, and he was dead of a heart attack before he could be forced into civilization.

Maybe the search's end should have been a warning that one day men might realize optimism could only get them so far. Once every group of people, no matter how remote or disinterested in the rest of the world they had been, were declared to be affected by the same disorder, it should have been obvious that better days weren't possible. Maybe the day that lone man from the jungle died, a man who strove his entire life to get away from other men, only to be scared to death by them, was the day the first ember of that fire actually started.

For people like Jeffrey, even the appearance of babies born into silence, an end that could finally be seen in the distance, didn't mean life had to be complicated. In some ways, life had become simpler. Sure, there were some new worries, but they were counterbalanced by the slew of traditional concerns that faded away. Crooked politicians, global warming, national debts—all of it became irrelevant. On the nights he sat outside on the porch with his son, it was impossible for Jeffrey to see the Blocks as ever possibly being a bad thing.

Ever since Galen's birth, father and son had sat together on the chairs facing the street just the way they had in generations past. There were no children outside yelling or playing anymore, though. No deliverymen made their daily rounds. Barely a sound bounced off the sidewalks or ran through the back alleys. This time of day brought with it a unique stillness that was impossible not to enjoy. It was that special part of the evening, only lasting for a couple of minutes, when everyone was home from work, either eating supper or sitting around after the fact. The dogs were sleeping following their dinners too.

Only the birds, hidden in the trees, continued offering beeps and blurts, reassurances that the world had not come to a complete stop. The flock's hiccupped chorus allowed Jeffrey a chance to close his eyes and completely forget where he was, and, for a moment, even who he was. It was during these minutes of silence over the years that his job seemed tolerable, that he stopped worrying about what the next day would bring for him and his family, that he managed not to worry about anything really.

Then, after the momentary intermission, in which only the birds tried to make peace with the world, the noises slowly came back. A car horn would honk. A neighbor would yell at his TV. It always happened. And each night, when it did happen, Jeffrey was brought back to the porch and to his quiet, sweet Galen.

Somewhere off in the distance, a dog started barking. The birds were startled into silence. Almost immediately, a slurred voice yelled that somebody better shut the animal up or he would shut it up himself.

Jeffrey opened his eyes, sighed, and began talking to Galen again. He squinted across the street to see inside their neighbor's front window. There were no lights on anywhere in the house, and the curtains were still apart.

"Looks like the Becks left last night," he said.

Most likely they had packed whatever they held dear and driven south to Washington to join the others. If they left before everyone else, they could have their pick of vacant apartments in Dupont Circle or near the White House.

He leaned back against his wicker chair before adding, "Thank God they didn't burn their house down before they left."

If he said the same thing to Katherine she would give him a light nudge and comment that it was that same cynicism which had made her fall in love with him. If he said the same thing to his mother she would tell him he needed to learn to be happy for other people. His father would simply grunt, neither agreeing nor disagreeing. But his son, his son would never offer those responses or any others.

Jeffrey looked over at his boy. Galen was in the exact same position he had been in since being wheeled onto the porch. There were no stifled yawns in which the boy—the young man—tried to hide his impatience so he could get back inside and watch the rest of the game. There was no irritation that he had to spend each evening with his father on the porch rather than going out with his friends or girlfriend. Jeffrey leaned over to make sure his son didn't have saliva forming at the corner of his mouth. More importantly, he inhaled to make sure Galen was still accident-free. It was always a pleasant treat when they could get through this ritual without the air becoming foul; the nights they had to go back inside early to get Galen cleaned off were the same nights Jeffrey went to bed irritated, feeling like the day had been a waste.

The dog's echoing bark sounded again. Then a growl, not the dog's but a man's, and an empty beer bottle shattering. Another slurred threat followed: the next bottle would hit the dog instead of sailing over its head.

Jeffrey sighed before looking at his son again. Every once in a while Galen would blink. There was never a reason for this. It wasn't because of an eyelash or because a fly tickled his eyebrow. Other than this blinking, the eyes remained still, never wavering from side to side, never focusing on new things. They didn't even scan for where the drunken man's threat had come from. His son had been born without the ability to know what was happening in the world around him, not even understanding his father was there to protect him. Every child born after Galen was the same way.

In the years prior to the Great De-evolution, Jeffrey and Katherine had talked about having three or four children. Galen wound up being their only child—one of the many times Jeffrey had a plan that the world laughed away with a shrug. By the time Galen was born, there wasn't even a remote possibility that their next child could be any different.

"Beautiful night," Jeffrey said to his son. And it was true. They were surrounded by rows of houses, but the sycamore and the small flower garden made him feel like he was separated from everything else. "Maybe we'll head south too. What do you think of that?"

He smiled at his boy. Galen's breathing was always perfectly steady and low. It reminded Jeffrey of the wind pushing gently against the trees—never a violent thunderstorm or a completely still day, but always the reassurance that kept the leaves awake. While Jeffrey was clearing his throat more often than he used to, a sign of old age, his son never rasped or choked for a next breath. Nor did the breathing ever stop completely. It was a calming thing to be around.

When the dog barked again, the drunken man yelled, "Shut that damn animal up. I'm warning you."

Jeffrey reached out and took Galen's hand in his palm. The other thing that made Jeffrey smile each time he inspected his son was how much Galen looked exactly like a version of himself from thirty years earlier. Before the grey hair started to appear. Before wrinkles formed where his eyes squinted when he smiled. Jeffrey's face could be cut out of the wedding photos with Katherine, a picture of Galen inserted in his place, and no one would ever know. They had the same stubby nose and dark eyes, the same thick eyebrows and ear lobes. There was nothing that could make a father more proud of his son than those enduring resemblances. The simplicity of looking alike, of passing down a solid jaw line, dark hair, and yes, even hairy arms, tapped into something universal, something permanent, that no other achievement could rival. Any time Jeffrey wanted to he could see a reminder of what he had looked like when he first met Katherine, a younger version of himself always by his side to show him which path his life was taking. That by itself, even if there was nothing else between them, was enough for him to love Galen as much as any father loved any son.

Sitting there, he wondered if he might feel the same way if he ran into someone else on the street that looked just like him. Surely not. But if not, why did he devote himself to Galen so much? There were certainly no other shared experiences that linked Jeffrey with his son. Growing up, Galen had never asked if it was OK to sleep in his parents' bed after having a nightmare. He had never thrown a baseball with his dad, never asked for advice with girls. These nights together were the only thing they had, the two of them sitting on the porch, Jeffrey always doing the talking, Galen always the listening. The world was full of other activities to take part in and full of other people to take part in them with—wasn't that what life was all about?—yet through all of the silence Jeffrey loved his son more than anything else in the world.

And how unfair was it to Katherine that she could never be loved in greater proportion than their son, even though she kept Jeffrey sane, kept him smiling and optimistic, while Galen offered nothing but silence? Jeffrey's memories of Galen were limited to cleaning him at night, brushing his teeth, changing his clothes, and wheeling him out to the porch each evening. The two loves shouldn't be comparable, yet they were.

The dog's next bark was immediately followed by another beer bottle shattering in the distance. Jeffrey strained to hear where the noise was coming from. His hearing, though, wasn't what it used to be. What was next? His eyes? His nose?

The dog kept barking and barking. It was a matter of time until the drunken man issued another threat. Without realizing he had done so, Jeffrey leaned forward as though his stomach hurt. The raucous dog had not only blotted out the birds, it had broken the tranquility of the night. But it was just a dog being a dog, scared of something or thinking it was protecting its owner. Both were parts of life: being scared, trying to protect the ones you loved. Jeffrey could attest to that. In fact, it was nice to have the old, familiar noise one more time—a random dog causing random sounds. That and a house and family were, after all, the American Dream.

It reminded Jeffrey of the days when he cursed neighborhood children under his breath because they always seemed to be yelling and laughing louder than he thought should be allowed. He hadn't been unruly when he was a child; his parents wouldn't have tolerated it. But then the children grew up and there were no other children to replace them. Other neighborhood noises, the rush-hour traffic and the trains taking cargo to other cities, disappeared over time as well. It was the disappearance of ice cream trucks and their jingles, of school buses slowing down every other vehicle on the road, of door-to-door salesmen pestering him with their wares. He couldn't recall the last time he had seen any of it.

The dog's barking burst into a yelp and then a squeal. In one step Jeffrey was at the edge of the porch. The same instincts that made him stand for action caused his fingers to curl into fists.

"I told you to shut that damn dog up," the same voice said from far up the street, the words slightly gurgled.

The more Jeffrey strained to hear where the unfamiliar voice had come from, the more it seemed to echo at him from every direction. Soon, he couldn't be sure if the voice had come from further up the street or from down the road near the highway. It might have been from the houses behind him or it could have been in front of him on one of the next blocks.

Even as recently as ten years ago, he would have recognized whoever's voice it was and could have talked things out with his neighbor. Now, half of the houses that still had people living in them belonged to those who had filtered down from New York or Boston. The newcomers didn't care about being polite because they knew it was only a matter of time until the next migration south. When all you lived for was the next place to call home, being courteous to your neighbors was no longer a priority.

Part of him wanted to take Galen back inside before wandering the neighborhood for the dog. When he found it he would whisper soothing coos until it trusted him, then he would pet it behind its ears. Once the animal forgot about the abuses that could be unfairly dealt, Jeffrey would tell it to have a good night and to be safe. Then he would start a new search, this time for the man. If things went well, the drunk would get a warning. In his younger days, a black eye or a broken nose might have been given as well.

The dog's owner was most likely gone, probably to Washington if not to someplace even further south. The dog would become yet another stray animal that Jeffrey would leave water for, another furry escort as he took his son around the neighborhood in his wheelchair for fresh air. Each time he saw one of these abandoned animals, his heart broke. They had been man's best friend one day, but the next they were left to fend for themselves. Forgotten because they were a hassle.

"God damn it," the drunken man yelled after yet another bark. "If that dogs barks one more time—" immediately, the dog barked again and Jeffrey laughed, appreciating its sense of humor. The drunken man growled and yelled that the dog was dead.

"You touch that dog," Jeffrey screamed, "and I'll kill you. You hear me? I'll kill you." He had to wipe his mouth when he was done yelling.

Before the Blocks appeared, someone might call the police and a pair of men in uniforms might show up and ask Jeffrey if everything was OK. These days, however, no men in blue would arrive. Not tonight, not tomorrow, not ever.

Jeffrey returned to his seat. “I’m really sorry you had to hear that,” he said to Galen.

A moment later, Katherine came to the front door and asked what all the noise was about. Instead of explaining what she heard or what she might have thought she heard, he simply apologized and squeezed her hand.

She rubbed the back of his neck the way he loved. “It’s time to come back inside.”

“It got dark out when I wasn’t paying attention.”

“Funny how that happens,” she said before telling him she loved him.

He handed his cup of coffee to her so she could carry it while he turned the wheelchair around and brought their son back indoors.

With Galen in bed, they watched the news for a couple of minutes. When that quickly became too depressing, they flipped to a current events show, but that wasn’t much better than the real news.

There was a story of a man in Great Falls, Montana, who had been in a coma for twenty years because of a motorcycle accident. Month after month, year after year, the man was stashed away in a back ward of the hospital. Piles of motionless bodies collected around the comatose patient. As time went by, however, more and more Blocks were being transferred to group homes.

One day, as another group of abandoned Blocks

were transported from the hospital to their permanent resting spot—a gutted high school—the comatose man was accidentally taken with them. The mistake was an easy one to make: his IV looked just like a Block's nutrient tube. Used to inanimate bodies, none of the workers gave a second thought to this man being twice the age of the others. To make matters worse, the man's family had already gone south to Boise, so he wasn't missed by anyone when he disappeared from the hospital. For two years, the unconscious man received all of the care, food, and hydration he would ever need because the caretakers treated him as if he were just another Block.

But then, the man in the coma, as people in comas will occasionally do, woke up out of the blue. Video surveillance of the Block shelter showed one of the bodies sitting up from the cot where it had been lying perfectly still for two years.

There were, unfortunately, no caretakers around at the moment the comatose man woke up. If there had been, they could have explained the world to him. Instead, as he collected himself, he realized he was surrounded by thousands of motionless bodies. There's no telling what he thought had happened to the world in the blank space between losing control of his motorcycle and opening his eyes in a gymnasium where track and field banners were still hanging from the rafters. All he knew was that the entire world was made up of bodies hooked up to feeding tubes. He quickly went insane.

First, he tore the IV from his arm. Then he stumbled to the closest fire alarm, set it off, and disappeared into a stairwell. No firefighters responded to the alarm; they had already vacated the city. No one caught up to the man in time to explain that aliens weren't enslaving us for food, or whatever scenario his mind had conjured up. The man, completely unaware that the Great De-evolution was talking place, that he was surrounded by Blocks rather than by mindless bodies harvested for some nefarious purpose, got in the first car he found and drove it straight into a wall at ninety miles per hour. He flew through the windshield and was instantly killed.

Everyone who watched the story that night would undoubtedly have nightmares of falling asleep one day, the world seemingly normal, and then opening their eyes to find everyone around them completely motionless and quiet.

"Why bother turning the TV on at all if this is what they're going to show us?" Jeffrey said, but Katherine didn't say anything.

With the TV off, the room became dark.

"Remember how nervous we were when we first found out I was pregnant?" she said.

He took her hand in his. "Seems like a long time ago. Like a different life."

She put her head against his shoulder. "I love you more every day."

Later in the night, he went back to the front door to make sure the dog wasn't barking or that the man wasn't wandering the streets looking for it. The streetlights hummed and made everything on the ground look slightly yellow, slightly sick. The street was still. The dog was sleeping somewhere where it felt safe. The neighbor was snoring off the alcohol and would wake up with a hangover. Both would be back the next day, both getting along as best as they knew how. And Jeffrey would take his son back out on the porch the next evening and the evening after that, and they would sit together and listen to the birds for those special few minutes of peace.

**

The fire behind him, still engulfing the remains of everything that had once been inside the stadium, Jeffrey continued his walk back to the base. The nights on the porch with Galen seemed like they must have been a part of someone else's life.

His mind was blank. Every once in a while he looked back at the smoke. How could there be a giant fire in the middle of the city? He was more confused by it—a ball of flames certainly didn't belong there—than he was alarmed. But each time he turned and looked, it was still there.

Cars continued to pass him on their way toward the disaster. He didn't notice them anymore, though. A silver Mercedes almost hit Jeffrey without the driver ever noticing. His mind had slowed until it was only able to process two things: getting back to the base, and wondering how a giant fire could be burning in the middle of the city.

By the time he got back to Fort Dix the conference room was empty. The lights were off. Instead of a retirement party for one person, a going away celebration for the entire base had been taking place. Empty beer cans were strewn around the expensive room. Cake and icing were smeared across the dry-erase board. No one cared anymore. The revelers left it that way knowing it was their final day on the job. Their superiors were all gone and nothing they did mattered. The conference room, with its giant hand-carved oak table and array of flat screen TVs, had once been the pride and joy of the men on base. Now, beer was spilled all over the floor, where ants gulped it up until they were drunk and drowning. Some of the men had used the cake's icing to turn the luxurious conference room into the inside of a bathroom stall. A finger-painted message, in delicious blue creamy sugar, said, "General Bay liked dick". Red icing was smeared to offer a Bible verse that Jeffrey wasn't familiar with. White icing was smeared to read, "It was the best of times. It was the worst of times."

He went past empty offices, one after another, remembering the different people who had sat at each desk throughout the years. When he flipped on the lights to his office he was greeted with the same giant mound of boxes that tormented him day after day, each one filled with fifty pounds of outdated forms and receipts.

He thought about taking the boxes to the nearest window so he could watch them explode on the concrete two stories below, paper bursting everywhere. The entire base would be covered in the uselessness of carbon copies, faxes, and printouts. Maybe a piece of paper would get carried away by the wind until it got stuck in the bumper of a truck heading south, or maybe a piece would stick to the foot of a man heading on board a vessel to Europe. The possibilities were endless. The realities, however, were as painful as what the world offered every day: most of it would eventually collect against the base fences. Some would become additional garbage gathered at the already polluted pond just off base.

Out the window, the smoke was taking over the entire sky.

A random thought made him think of Galen then, but when he thought of his son, he envisioned the boy sitting at home where he always was.

Without thinking, he picked up one of the boxes and launched it through the window. The lid came off in mid-flight. Half the paper was floating away in the wind before the box even hit the ground.

It was only then, when he turned to sit down again, that he saw Lieutenant Griggs sitting in his corner office, staring out the doorway to see what Jeffrey was doing. The man must have been sitting there in the quiet the entire time.

"Don't worry about it," Griggs said. "I think General Bay would have been more irritated about the writing on the conference room wall. If he was still here, that is."

"What are you doing here?" Jeffrey asked, the only thing he could think to say.

Griggs didn't reply, only turned back to face his desk and the family photos arranged there. Griggs, he knew, had a Block daughter two years older than Galen. The man took one of the framed pictures in his hands and, without turning around to face Jeffrey, held it up so it could be seen. In the picture, Griggs was wearing khaki shorts and a Hawaiian shirt on the beach. His wife and Block daughter were lying in hammocks on either side of him.

The black cloud was hovering over the entire city now. There was a good chance Griggs's daughter was there. He didn't ask about Jeffrey's son and Jeffrey didn't ask about the man's child.

"Was your wife near the stadium?" Jeffrey said.

"No!" Griggs snapped around to face Jeffrey as if a threat had been issued. But then the man had a flicker of recognition, maybe remembered the day Jeffrey had brought Galen to work on what had ended up being the very last "Bring Your Child To Work" day. "No," Griggs said again. Then, "But my brother was. He thought of Stacey as his own daughter…" Griggs put his face in his hands and shook.

What could Jeffrey say that would make anything better? It wasn't worth trying to joke about how much it might cheer the man up if he threw useless boxes of useless paper out the window.

"What are you going to do?"

"Hang out here for a while," Griggs said. "Collect myself."

"I meant in two days, for the city's relocation."

"Oh, we've all been planning to go. I'll still go."

"You'd still go there with your brother? Like nothing happened?"

Griggs didn't say anything else. Only stared blankly at the picture of his daughter.

From the window, Jeffrey could see some of the papers swirling around on the ground. Griggs put the picture of his family back on the desk before offering a nervous laugh, the type of hysterical laugh someone would give if they had a gun to their head with someone telling them to be happy or else have their face blown off.

Jeffrey shifted from one foot to the other. "Do you know where the keys are for Hangar 3?"

The other man shrugged.

"Take care of yourself, Griggs," Jeffrey said, but the only response he received was another shrug.

Before leaving, he looked back one more time. Griggs was still there, still sitting at his desk without picking up the phone or doing anything at all, simply sitting there as if that would allow time to freeze and keep anything else from happening.

Jeffrey didn't see anyone else on his walk to the hangar. Its main door, large enough to accommodate the planes, tanks, and whatever else might be inside, was closed, but the side entrance, miniature in comparison, was unlocked. With the lights off, only the outlines of the giant machines could be made out. With the click of a switch, however, a series of overhead lights revealed a selection of green, grey, and camouflage metal.

There were no planes in the hangar. Jeffrey had no idea if they were someplace else on base or if someone had already taken them for other purposes. He saw two helicopters, three tanks, and one Humvee. A single golf cart was parked in the corner. It too was painted camouflage as though that would help it be taken more seriously. With another flip of a switch, the hangar doors rumbled to life and the enclosure opened to the world.

Everything in the hangar, even the helicopters, was to be used in the migration south. Strangely, nothing made the citizens feel more comforted about their upcoming journey than armored machines of war.

But, Jeffrey thought, they could handle having one less tank to lead the charge south. The same group that had set fire to the stadium, letting part of its population burn with it, would have to do without. He noticed a tarp strewn on the ground where another vehicle had been parked until recently. There was no telling where the transport was now. It was possible that a military Jeep was currently making its way down Interstate 95 on the way to Florida, a family trying to get away from the madness before everyone else. It was also possible the vehicle was sitting at the bottom of Colliers Lake with a drowned Colonel still sitting inside, an empty bottle of whiskey in the seat next to him.

In all of his years in the military, Jeffrey had never actually been inside a tank. But then again, he had also never fought in a war, jumped out of a plane, really, done anything related to actually protecting the country. In front of one of the machines at last, he was surprised at how much bigger it was than he thought it would be. He envisioned an oversized Oldsmobile elevated on motorized tracks. What he saw was more like a fortress traveling on a conveyor belt. He tapped the metal body with his knuckles. There was barely a sound at all.

At first he thought he might jump up to the tracks, then to the hull. Instead, his knuckles ached as he pulled himself up the side of the tread, his knees scraping over the nuts and bolts as he righted himself. In basic training he had been able to climb a thirty-foot rope without using his legs. Now, he grunted as he hoisted himself up the side of the machine.

His shoes clacked against the metal as he walked to the turret and the hatch. He looked down inside of what was, essentially, a moveable cave. He could climb down into the dark, climb back out to see the daylight whenever he wanted, but this cave could also transport him across the broken roads. This armored rock could move him anywhere he wanted.

And with that thought, he lowered himself inside. Unsure of what to expect, he partly assumed it would look like a jet's cockpit. But the controls in front of him didn't seem that complicated: a steering lever, a speed lever, a brake pedal, a clutch. Nothing he couldn't handle.

The engine came alive on the first try. Part of him had expected the tank not to start up at all as if sensing he wasn't the type of person who should be driving it. Another misconception was that he expected it to be as loud as a jet, that he would need industrial strength headphones to block out the noise, but it was similar in volume to a riding lawn mower—if the riding lawn mower could crush cars and go through brick walls.

He pulled a lever, pushed a pedal, and took a deep

breath. The machine lurched backwards. He kept the turret door open as the tank made its way out of the hangar.

The black sky was spreading. The infection now covered every part of the city's outline and was continuing to the surrounding parks and suburbs. And more smoke was still pouring up into the sky, the sickness spreading as far as the eye could see. Surely, given time, it would spread all the way to the ocean before enveloping the entire world.

Griggs was staring out the window at him as the tank rumbled by. The two men looked at each other for a moment, but neither waved goodbye or smiled. Two days later, Griggs would get in his SUV with his wife and his brother and his brother's wife and they would all head to Washington together, trapped by the silence of not being able to discuss why their children weren't with them.

The tank rumbled past the front gate. No longer was there base security checking your ID on the way on and off the government grounds. Years earlier, when the base was fully functional, they had even had speed traps set up around the roads. Anyone going faster than fifteen miles per hour would have gotten pulled over by the unsmiling pseudo police.

Instead of turning west to go back to the city, toward the flames, the tank turned east, toward the ocean. Jeffrey was aware of his actions enough to know he was driving away from the city, but he never really gave thought to the fact that he was actually leaving it. He didn't think about his son's dead body because, somewhere in his head, he still envisioned his son at home on the porch, enjoying the silence. Before long, the tank approached the Garden State Parkway. Instead of heading south toward Washington, where everyone else would be going in two more days, he took the ramp north. Fort Dix got smaller and smaller as he drove away.

The newness of driving a tank made him feel like he was flying down the road on a go-cart. In reality, he was only going twenty miles per hour. He kept it that speed until he felt like there was no way the black cloud could descend on him. If it rained, he was sure that black liquid would pour down on him and suffocate him too.

The entire first day of driving, he looked back at the cloud of smoke as though expecting it to catch up to him, overtake him, and then kill everything ahead. It must be visible from Washington and New York. Maybe people over seas were wondering if a different type of madness, something other than the slow decline of mankind, had come over the Americans. Maybe the final astronauts were seeing it from outer space and were wondering what in the hell was happening.

Once he was finally away from it, he slowed the tank even more. He would continue at that casual pace for the rest of his journey. There was no point going faster; he had nowhere he had to be and no schedule for when he had to be there.

He merely focused on avoiding abandoned cars on the road. He was still too overwhelmed with fleeing the smoke, being inside a tank, traveling on a deserted highway, to think about his son. And even when he did think of Galen, he didn't think of him at the epicenter of the flames, but, as though nothing tragic had happened, at home.

And then, with even more black smoke rising up into the sky, he closed the hatch door, and continued north. That was all.

Chapter 3

"Whether you like it or not, the calls are getting louder for us to leave this city."

Two men sat facing each other in front of studio cameras. The more fiery of the two men made a habit of wearing pinstripe suits that exaggerated just how tall and skinny he was. Along with sunken cheeks, he bore a striking resemblance to a smug Grim Reaper.

"Why isn't anyone stepping up to help us?" he asked into the camera. "Do they want us to just sit here until it's too late and we're all dead?" He had been saying the same thing for two years.

After the disaster in Boston, the remains of an entire stubborn city frozen to death in a terrible blizzard, it was easy to see the importance of moving south where there were still enough people to keep the infrastructure functioning properly. It had been four years since New York sent a delegation up to see why no one had heard from the Boston settlement following the harsh winter. Frozen bodies were everywhere. The city's workers had already left. Without them, the roads didn't get plowed. People were stuck in their houses. The power generators, designed to make each house self sufficient, began killing entire families due to carbon monoxide poisoning. Worse yet, the generators at the group home in the Boston Garden failed. Most people went to sleep shivering underneath green championship banners, then never woke up again. The stories of what had been found there were enough for New York to join up with Philadelphia earlier than planned.

It was amazing, though, how quickly the houses around Jeffrey, temporarily infused with people wearing Yankees hats, would start to empty again. A family would leave in the middle of the night to join their relatives in Florida. An elderly couple would pass away. Someone would finally succumb to cancer. Each day a few more people were gone, without new children to replace them, and after three years the city was once again reminding them how empty a metropolis could feel.

As if to exacerbate people's fears as they watched the gradual decline in population, protests were held each week to make people even more afraid. Half the protests were organized by groups that were frustrated with the lack of planning for how to get the entire city relocated to Washington. The other protests were to complain about having thousands of people to take along for the ride who couldn't otherwise take care of themselves. On bad days, both protests occurred at the same time and the two masses of people combined into a scared mob looking for someone to blame.

But there were still people who said everything would be OK. There was no need for panic. Jeffrey was one of them.

"These are trying times," the other man on TV said. "But we have to make sure we have the resources necessary for the trip if we're going to pick up and move everyone a hundred miles south. You can't just do something like that at the drop of a hat. You need to plan. Especially with the roads the way they are."

The man in pinstripes sighed and rolled his eyes. "If it was up to you we would still be planning the trip to Washington after everyone there had already packed up and gone down to Raleigh."

Jeffrey had to hand it to the skeleton—he had a way

of helping people realize they were disgusted or horrified when they hadn't previously known it; he had a way of getting already irritated people to yell out their windows that they weren't going to take it anymore.

The screen went black.

"Why do you insist on watching that stuff?" Jeffrey said to Katherine, the remote still in his hand. "It just makes you worry."

He had to admit, though, that this show was better than most of what was left for entertainment. Twenty years ago, there were more than forty radio stations available in the area. Now, there were only three still broadcasting live across the airwaves. A couple of stations, their doors already closed for the last time, kept a loop of songs playing over and over. Others had pre-recorded motivational speeches playing, intended to keep people's spirits up. The other stations became static. The only thing remaining were a handful of men bantering all day about the Blocks and what to do with them. One show was compassionate toward the silent army, but most of them, not realizing their time as shock jocks had already ended, spoke about using Blocks to fill the potholes in roads or for target practice. The last time Jeffrey ever listened to one of these shows, the host was laughing about wanting to use hundreds of motionless Block bodies to spell out HELP in giant letters so anyone watching from outer space would see it and know we were still fucked.

And yet, as bad as the radio could be, it wasn't as bad as the gangs roaming southern California. Without any new teens to recruit, their youngest members were now in their thirties. The bandana-wearing delinquents didn't bother with drive-by shootings anymore. Most of the members had moved into gated communities with cast-iron fences originally intended to keep their kind out. The fences were spray painted with symbols to let everyone else know exactly which gang was living in which celebrity's former mansion. No longer, though, did the gangs go around the rest of the city spray painting nonsense on brick walls and underpasses. No one had understood what things like "808" and "Squirrely 4 Ever" were supposed to mean anyway. To add insult to injury, a senior citizens' club in Los Angeles had seen a collection of graffiti at the old rec center and thought it was a beautiful way to liven up depressed people, so they started a club to paint every abandoned office building with happy images of Hokusai waves, Starry Nights, and even The School of Athens. The entire city was soon covered with graffiti that warmed everyone's heart. Gang symbols seemed foolish against such artistry.

That didn't stop the gangs from spreading their symbols, however. They were just spread in a different way: Blocks were being found all around the city with insignias tattooed on their foreheads. A Block's family would turn their backs at a park, or even in their own backyard, just long enough for a group of forty-year old thugs to kidnap the motionless body, drive the Block around the neighborhood in a van, before dropping them back off. The only difference was that the Block had a fresh tattoo, inked in the gang's colors, right on their forehead.

In Chicago, before the city was evacuated, two rival gangs competed for how many new members they could get. The Great De-evolution was in full swing, so the only new members were Blocks. Gangs made daily raids on the Block shelters to kidnap the biggest and meanest looking Blocks they could find. The mannequin-like bodies were dressed up in the gang's colors. But the Blocks never learned fancy gang signs. They never stole or robbed. They couldn't even sell drugs. Really, all they did was sit in rooms, all dressed in the same color clothing, doing nothing at all. Needless to say, aging gang members didn't want to be babysitters; the contest ended a month after it started, and the newly indoctrinated members were all returned to the Block shelters from which they had been stolen.

Aging populations still needed their drugs, but the dealers were having as hard a time as everyone else when it came to adjusting to the changing world. When paper money became useless, a little baggie of pot that would have sold for twenty bucks would now cost whatever jewelry the buyer was wearing. After they realized jewelry meant as little as money, dealers started trading their drugs for the few things that still had some sort of value: real seafood instead of the food processor's version, spare batteries instead of the bulky power generators everyone was issued. If you wanted a lifetime supply of coke, it was going to cost you your beachfront property at one of the final settlements. The user, who used to be able to wake up each day to a view of the waves crashing, would relocate to a condo further in town, but they would be too stoned to care.

Katherine was still looking at the blank television screen. "I hate that you always turn the TV off. I feel like we might get left behind if we don't keep up on the news each night."

"That wasn't the news. It was something that gets off on pretending to be the news. Don't let them scare you."

Upstairs, Galen was already in his version of sleep. Katherine snuggled closer to her husband. Every day he told her not to worry, and every day he knew she was more concerned than the previous day.

"The guys on TV always say the same thing," he told her for the hundredth time. "And they're only on TV at all because they're good at making everything seem so incredibly urgent."

Her grip relaxed, but she still stared at the black box with glassy eyes that didn't really see anything. "How many other families are going to leave before we go too?" she said. "I hate feeling like we're going to wake up one morning and be the last people here."

The corner of his shirt was damp from where her face had rested on his shoulder.

"Honey"—he stroked her hair while he spoke—"we aren't being left behind. The Donaldsons and the Carters are gone, but—"

Her face came back into light when she spoke: "And the Lees, and the McCarthys, and the Sosas."

In her face, he saw thirty years of memories with her, saw their lives together in the sparkle of her eyes. Tiny wrinkles were starting to appear at the corners of her cheeks where the skin had once been smooth. Her hair had the tiniest hint of grey mixed in with the blonde.

"Look at everyone who's still here," he said, "not the people who have left. The Cunninghams are still here. So are the Crenches and the Kramers. If we leave in the middle of the night, we're no better than anyone else who's already gone. Wouldn't you rather go down with the caravan?" Before she had a chance to respond, he added, "We'll be fine."

A couple of minutes went by without either of them saying anything. When he looked down again she was asleep. Her eyes were twitching and she gave a light groan as if receiving bad news, but it was sleep nonetheless.

He still remembered the early days, back when Galen was a baby. The news reported on a mother who had drowned her four-year old child in the bathtub. The baby, who had been born before the first signs of the Great De-evolution, had wailed at the hospital like any other normal baby, but then the mother killed it and threw it in the forest. When asked why she did it, she told the police her baby had turned into a Block. No one, especially the police, believed her; she was arrested and sent to prison for the rest of her life. But when the story was told on the evening news, instead of mentioning her mile-long rap sheet, her history of child abuse, they made her sound like an unfairly treated, distraught mother who was trying to cope with her child's disease. Burglary, drug use, drug dealing, obstructing a police investigation—she had done it all. The only thing that was reported on the news, though, was that a mother said her healthy baby had suddenly become a Block.

Afterwards, there were similar stories every few months, with each one causing another wave of hysteria until people eventually regained their senses. No one wanted to believe bad things could happen to good people: "There must be a mistake! It's not the end of man, it's just a sickness!" Others liked blaming the silent masses for their problems even though a silent body, a motionless body, couldn't do anything to cause anyone any problems at all.

In Australia, a python suffocated a baby. In a crazy world, it made perfect sense that the parents refused to blame the python. Surely, they said, their baby would have cried for help as the monster wrapped itself around the baby's little body… unless it too had become a Block! People all around the world took their healthy children to the doctor's office to see if their child might be next.

The population found a way to blame any normal baby's death on it having turned into a Block. A normal baby was said to have turned into a Block baby right before it died in a house fire. No matter how many scientists said there were no confirmed cases of this, no matter how many autopsies disproved these theories, people went on believing the Blocks were victims of a sickness, a plague, rather than accepting that it was simply the way the world was working. Those dedicated to a life of faith told anyone who would listen: "God wouldn't create man just to have him go extinct this way. This has to be a mistake. There has to be something we can do!"

Just a year earlier, as Jeffrey ate his cereal next to Galen, a news report had recounted how a teenager was found inside the remains of an imploded convention center in New Orleans. News footage of the implosion showed a single silhouette standing on the sixth floor of the building, doing nothing but staring out the windows in the seconds leading up to the explosions. The news kept saying that the only reason someone would ignore all of the warnings, alarms, and the loud countdown to the detonation was if they had become a Block. Jeffrey had groaned and, as he always did, turned the TV off. But when he went to work that day one of the other officers was asking everyone what kind of chemicals were used in the construction of the convention center that might have caused someone to change from being a normal person to a Block. And how many other buildings had used those same chemicals?

Sliding away from his sleeping wife, he turned and walked down the hall to Galen's room. His son was in the same position as earlier, the same position he would be in when the morning arrived and Jeffrey and Katherine woke up. His boy's eyes were open, staring at the blank ceiling in a way that reminded Jeffrey of a dead body, so he leaned over and swiped his fingertips across them so they were closed again. Katherine never failed to chide him for continuing with the pointless motion—it was, after all, only for Jeffrey's own benefit—but he liked the feeling it gave him, even if it was false, that he could put his son to bed properly.

The boy's room was as different from Jeffrey's room when he was Galen's age as Jeffrey's room had been from his father's at the same age. But the changes weren't because of the times they lived in or the hobbies they enjoyed. Jeffrey's father had grown up with posters of sports stars on his walls while Jeffrey had posters of popular bands. But Galen had no hobbies. There were no singers he liked more than others. Nor were there any sports trophies or academic ribbons. Katherine had once said that a child's room without any memories or pictures wasn't a kid's room at all. What was it then, a sarcophagus? A day later, Jeffrey called in sick to work and spent the afternoon painting dignified stripes of blues and greens—a place holding life instead of a box waiting for its opposite. On two of the walls, he put up framed pictures of the three of them together. At least his son would have that much.

In these moments there was nothing, save the voice in the back of his head, that kept him from believing he had a normal son who could wake up at any minute and talk to him. When everything was silent and covered in darkness and his son was a vague outline, he could imagine the life he had always planned for rather than the one he was actually living. He imagined a son who had played high school sports, brought home report cards with good grades, asked for advice with girls. But life wasn't a fairytale, so he made a set of unwanted fantasies to counter-balance the blindly optimistic hopes: Galen breaking curfew, coming home drunk after parties, having his heart broken. These pains made the unabashed fantasies seem more realistic.

Yes, he would love to have a son who he could talk and laugh and fish with, but Galen also allowed him to bypass millions of arguments and a thousand times when son supposedly knew better than father. He was spared from suffering the times when Galen didn't want to be seen with him in public because no kid wanted to be seen with his parents at a young age.

Katherine's eyes were open when he got back to the living room. He thought she might ask what he had been doing, but she didn't say anything, and a couple of minutes later, both of them on the sofa instead of in their bed, he heard the raspy breath indicating she was once again asleep. In the dark, in the final few minutes before he went to sleep, he imagined what it would be like to have a son who might cry out in the middle of the night, who needed to be comforted after a nightmare. At twenty, Galen was too old to do these things now even if he was a normal child, which made Jeffrey ask himself if he would ever be able to stop envisioning this other life.

**

The tank rumbled on. At the exit for Route 9, he drove north toward the Garden State Parkway where he would once again proceed east. There was only a little more land available before he would run out of road and end up in the ocean. He drove with no more purpose than the simple thought, *Get away from the smoke*. He didn't think about getting away from Katherine or from the spot where his son had been burned alive because those things didn't seem real to him.

There were times in the tank when he didn't even believe Galen was actually dead. There must have been a misunderstanding; the boy was fine. Even as the ocean appeared, Jeffrey thought there had to be some kind of mistake for why so much smoke could be created in the middle of a city. Yes, there had been a giant fire, but in the confusion leading up to the match being struck, his son was probably skipped over, might not have been near the stadium at all. Maybe there hadn't actually been any Blocks inside the stadium. It simply wasn't possible that thousands of people would be purposefully burned to the ground.

As the Atlantic approached, he had half a mind to drive the tank straight into the oncoming waves until water poured in and the machine was stuck in the sand and the surf. Maybe then, as water drowned him inside the confines of the tank, he would wake up from this strange dream.

Three weeks earlier, on the news, there had been a story of a man who walked into a coffee shop, sipped his large mocha for a few minutes, then told everyone he was going down the street to the abandoned campus so he could wake up from his nightmare. The man seemed calm enough; none of the other customers paid him any attention. Thirty minutes later, a series of explosions sounded and the entire four-story academic building came crumbling down to the ground. A goodbye note at the man's home said he had been knocked out during a football game in the weeks leading up to the beginning of the Great De-evolution. He had become convinced that everything since then had all been part of a bad dream. What better way to wake up from a nightmare than with dynamite and tons of concrete crashing down on you?

That, too, could explain why a 747 crashed into a field outside Chicago a week earlier after making a lone circle around the city. Would someone traveling south assume Jeffrey had made the same decision if they saw his tank sitting a hundred yards off the beach with waves crashing all around it?

As sure as he was that there had been a colossal mistake—it was impossible to believe his son was anywhere but at home—he continued north after arriving at the beach. Katherine could have decided against taking their son to the stadium. Maybe she had been apologizing for ever having considered taking their son near the rally, not because she actually had. A thousand thoughts kept him believing Galen was still alive. Maybe Katherine was deceiving him, paying him back for something he had done. Maybe, maybe, maybe. Some of the thoughts didn't even make sense as he thought them, but the sheer number of doubts allowed him to believe Galen could be alive.

The tank came to a road that followed the shoreline. Back when he was a boy, these roads had been swarming with families. Now, even during summer, no cars lined the road except for those that had been abandoned. No families waited at the crosswalks for the light to change so they could cross the street and let their children run through the sand. The stoplights still functioned, though. Thirty seconds of red light ticked away until it was replaced by fifteen seconds of green.

At one intersection, as the tank passed under a red light, there was a flash, a camera clicked, and an automated system sent a picture of the tank to a now deserted government building where the license plate, if the tank had one, would be matched with Jeffrey's address so he could receive a ticket in two months. The juvenile side of him, the side he wasn't allowed to show very often after becoming a father, thought about turning the turret toward the camera and blowing it off the face of the earth. If he were younger he would stand up as the tank made its way through the red light sensor and stick his bare cheeks up at the camera. A photo of his hairy ass would forever sit in an abandoned office computer database.

The further he got from the highway, the fewer abandoned cars littered the roads. Each time he drove by an overpass for one of the main highways leading to the beach, he could look out the viewfinder and see long lines of cars scattered about like misplaced junkyards.

Only once did he pass by a road in which the abandoned cars were all lined up on the two right lanes so that traffic could easily pass on the other two lanes. Someone must have spent their entire day walking up and down that strip of highway, aligning the cars neatly. The cars were just going to sit there until they rusted into a slow oblivion. Jeffrey wanted to shake the fool by the shoulders and ask what the point was of making something pretty and organized anymore.

At the next overpass, someone had come along and set a string of cars on fire, presumably to see the line of fuel tanks explode like giant kernels popping. Just like that, the line of abandoned cars was turned into a singed wasteland.

Looking at the cars, he turned to say something to Galen, before realizing he was alone in the tank.

All of this had to be a mistake. Surely, Galen would have been at home when the fire started. How many times had he told Katherine everything would be OK?

The second beach town was as abandoned as the first. No families walked the boardwalk. No joggers ran for exercise and a tan. The distinct beach town smell of toffee and suntan lotion was gone. They were things he had never thought to miss until they weren't there anymore. People always talked about how Maine was officially void of human life, that New Hampshire was probably empty as well, along with Vermont, but the government kept delaying the official "Naturalized" status for those states so as to not cause more panic.

But people never talked about the little things that disappeared through all of it. The smells that vanished. The sounds. When was the last time he held a piece of vanilla fudge up to his mouth? When was the last time he heard a carousel's music as children were twirled in circles? Someone could come up and ask him what a beach town smelled like and he would have to shrug his shoulders and say, "Salt water?" It wasn't incorrect, but there was supposed to be so much more: cotton candy, cheap seafood snacks, spilt beer. None of that existed now. The seagulls tried to make up for it by providing tons and tons of bird shit. Everywhere he looked there were white spots of dried crap plastering the closed shops, the sidewalks, the burned-out neon signs.

At the first clear view of water, the tank came to a stop. His stomach growled at not receiving new food since breakfast. Hungry and thirsty, he left the tank and headed toward a small strip of abandoned restaurants. His throat was dry and sore. If he was going to make his way alone, he was going to have to take better care of himself.

The restaurants and stores were just like the houses: there was no need to take all of your possessions with you; there was plenty more of everything where you were going, and the resources themselves—the food, the clothes, the TVs or computers—weren't worth their weight. Each time another person died and there were fewer people in the world, material possessions also held less value. There would be a day when there were only two or three people left. At that point not even the *Mona Lisa* or the *Star of Africa* diamond would have any value. Everything was becoming worthless.

He grew up reading comic books that told about an apocalyptic future of gangs hoarding water, food, women, and whatever else they could find. The Great De-evolution was nothing of the sort. There was more clean drinking water than anybody would ever need. There was more food and clothes than people would ever be able to use up. Houses were abundant.

The first restaurant he stopped at still had pictures of celebrities who had dined there decades earlier. The walls were littered with smiling faces that had appeared in movies and TV shows. Everyone in the pictures looked happy.

In the kitchen, he found a supply of canned fruit and frozen meat that seemed as good as anything else. He could have walked next door and found different food there. One restaurant would probably have frozen seafood. Another might have pasta. But he was tired and hungry and wasn't picky about what he ate. He fired up the kitchen's stove and dropped the frozen chunk of meat on it.

Further north, he might have difficulty finding real food, but there would be food processors to keep him going. The Great De-evolution was no different from other disasters in that calamity had inspired technology. Refrigerators became popular in the early 1900s after food shortages led to starvation. The Atom Bomb came from WWII. The food processor came about when Blocks signaled man's impending end. Nearly any meal he wanted could be created by the machine, leaving him able to survive after farms stopped growing crops and grocery stores closed.

While he ate, he watched waves crash on the empty beach. The water boomed each time a wave broke, then swirled as it rushed back to meet the rest of the ocean. It was beautiful. Even after he was done eating he sat on top of the tank and watched the waves as if seeing them for the first time.

Of course, watching the waves made him think about Galen too. He had loved taking his son to the beach so they could sit in the quiet and watch the water flow onto the sand. Sometimes when he brought his son here, Jeffrey had spent the time recounting whatever he knew about the great body of water and the fish it contained, as if it were possible for him to teach his boy about the world. Other times, he was content to sit with his son, without saying anything at all, until Katherine woke from her nap or was ready for dinner.

Galen *had* to be home. He had to be safe. He had to be.

After eating a second plate of steak and fruit, his belly felt like it might burst. He took the dirty plate back to the restaurant's kitchen even though he could have left it in the dining area and no one would have cared. For his sanity's sake, he even cleaned it and left it to dry. It was important to keep up habits or else he could lose his mind very quickly. If he left the plate out in the open, he might as well piss on the street too. And if he did that, he might as well do whatever else he wished. It wouldn't be long before he had no rules to follow and his mind didn't know the difference between right and wrong.

He imagined Galen being there with him to see the waves crash one more time. Katherine would have chided him for not putting a stronger suntan lotion on their son before taking him outside.

The thoughts lingered even as the tank lurched forward and made its way north again.

Chapter 4

"Flint, Michigan had no issues when they relocated and joined up with Detroit. Why should we be any different?"

"Flint? Are you serious? Flint?" The Grim Reaper's laughter got him sitting up straight. "Flint? You really crack me up."

"You can laugh," his adversary said, already beginning to perspire. "But other cities have done it and they haven't had any problems. We'll be just fine. There's nothing to worry about."

"Did Flint have as many Blocks as us?"

"How would I know? I don't have those numbers."

"That's right, you don't know."

Jeffrey motioned to Katherine. "Turn it off. I can't listen to these guys today."

But instead of turning the TV off, she merely changed the station. An hour-long program was airing that would be translated into twenty different languages and be viewed by more than a billion people around the world. If the population wasn't in the second phase of decline, the estimated amount of people watching it would have beaten the final Super Bowl.

On the show, a collection of former spies met in a university auditorium to discuss what they had been doing before the Great De-evolution, confess to what was real and what was fiction, and provide an update on what former spies were doing now that there was no need for intelligence agencies. Seated in an oval, facing the audience, were intelligence officers from England, France, Israel, America, Russia, and China. A man had tried to attend as the official representative from North Korea but no one thought him to be sane, and everyone had a good laugh at the nonsense he might have said if given a microphone.

Each man attended the symposium with the understanding that they were now retired and, although they had all signed confidentiality agreements with their respective governments saying they would either be executed or spend the rest of their lives in jail if they gave away classified information, that rules of secrecy were no longer necessary by default because there was no need anymore to recruit double agents or disseminate misinformation. And, most importantly, nearly all of the governments they had once collected intelligence for were now defunct.

None of the men bothered to wear suits. None of them cared enough about ensuring the other men around them, all supposed trained assassins, had been patted down or walked through a metal detector, lest a poison dart launch from the side of a wristwatch or poison gas be released from a belt buckle. If those things had actually ever occurred, they were part of a different life. The moderator was a former college professor who had taught political science for three decades before this year's final graduating class signaled that he too was joining the ranks of unnecessary professionals.

"I still laugh," the English officer said, pointing to the French officer, "about the time our chaps planted the story in the news about your President nearly dying from diarrhea. There was absolutely nothing to gain from it, my good man, except shits and giggles."

The audience laughed. The other men on stage chuckled as well. The French officer could do nothing but pick imaginary lint from his shirt.

The Russian representative claimed to have had at least three different officers from each rival agency on his payroll. A brief round of bickering ensued when every other man claimed the same thing. The moderator asked what the point was to all of the secrets, double-crossing, and espionage, if every agency had men on the inside of every other agency.

The Chinese officer cleared his throat. “They didn’t have agents in every agency,” the man said.

When the intelligence officer from the United States and Russia started to protest, the Chinese representative pulled out a tablet for reference. “Yes, we knew about the men you had on your payroll in Beijing, Hangzhou, and Xi’an,” he said to the American. “And the men you were paying from Guangzhou, Shanghai, and Hong Kong,” he said to the Russian. “But we don’t count them because we were the ones who told them to start accepting money from you. It went into our party fund and paid for some nice lunch celebrations, but the men only fed you what we wanted them to.”

The American and the Russian sank back in their chairs without further protest.

The Israeli officer told the audience that the important thing, looking back, wasn’t what they had heard over the years, because that was just what the various agencies had wanted you to hear. “The things you hear about, even about our greatest blunders, was misinformation. We leaked stories of bungled assassination attempts to divert attention away from the fact that we had a computer transferring half of Iran’s economy into a secret fund.”

The English representative tried to say that the famous Rand fiasco, a drunken MI6 officer found sitting in a pool of his own urine in a French phone booth, was also a diversion tactic, but the French officer cut him off: "That was just a case of an Englishman who drank like a girl and pissed himself like a boy."

The American officer thought this was hilarious and reached over to give the French officer an awkward high-five.

At first, the ribbing was good-natured, but after twenty minutes the men's competitive spirit, if not remnants of their patriotism, started to surface. The Russian accused the American of backing out of a deal to share intelligence obtained from China. The Chinese representative said he already knew everything being given out to both countries. The Israeli officer made a bet with the man from China that he had a man on the inside who no one else knew about. The Englishman ruined the game by saying the spy's name before the Israeli or Chinese could. The French representative said that was the first time MI6 actually knew something useful.

The American said he wasn't sure why someone from France was even in attendance: "Did you guys actually do anything, or were you laughing at the paychecks you managed to collect?"

The French officer, tired of being belittled, left the stage. But before he did, he told the audience, "The CIA killed Kennedy. Every man on stage right now knows this as fact." Then he gave the other men the middle finger and walked off.

The crowd, this was being held in London, booed him ferociously as he left.

He paused before stepping off the stage and

disappearing behind a curtain. "Just so you all know," the Frenchman added, "for the last fifty years our country has had three missiles, each nuclear ready, with a hundred times more payload than the ones that hit Hiroshima and Nagasaki, aimed at your little island. And we fixed the result of ten different Manchester United versus Chelsea matches. And if you ever bother to look inside Shakespeare's tomb you'll notice it's empty. We took his remains as a joke, and you were all too stupid to realize it, so we kept them."

And with that, the man from France was gone.

The Chinese representative scanned some information on the tablet he was holding before saying, "Everything the French gentleman just said is factually accurate."

The moderator asked the men what life was like now that there were no longer any secrets to keep.

The Russian attendee, not wanting to have all of the wonderment stolen by the man from China, said, "Vot makes you think there are no more programs?" It was obvious he just wanted the respect of the audience, that he wasn't used to being outplayed in a room. "The spy game is never over. Even now, even this night, ve have been collecting intelligence. Russia never stops. Russia never forgets. You formed a blockade to obstruct our boats," he said to one of the men. "Ve never forget! A time vill come, before the end, ven retribution is paid. Maybe it vill be a year from now. Maybe it von't be until you are all old men, ready to die anyway, but ve vill have the last laugh. The spy game is never over."

The moderator asked if this payback would come in the form of nuclear war, a chemical attack, or something else, but the Russian, disappearing behind the same curtain the French man had disappeared behind, was already signaling for his cab to be called. The audience, both in the auditorium and at home, was left to wonder if evil, scheming men were still out there, still power hungry, still plotting away in secret.

Of course the threat would upset Katherine.

The screen went blank. Jeffrey asked what her plans were for the next day, mainly because if there was silence, she would imagine what the men on TV would have said next, and in a way, letting her think of the possibilities was worse than if she actually watched the show.

"I don't know. I guess pack another box of stuff to take down to Washington."

"You know," he said, "we won't have much room in the truck when we head south."

She pulled away from him, and he didn't say anything else.

Katherine said, "Do you remember what it was like when we were young? Our biggest responsibility was going to class and taking quizzes. Our biggest worry was getting a good grade on the next test."

One day they had been carefree teenagers without a genuine worry in the world. Each year had added another concern, however. Eventually, they were a married couple with daily responsibilities that they couldn't have fathomed as young adults. After being married for a while, the endless debates had started about whether or not they were ready to become parents. Then the Blocks appeared and the discussion took a more urgent tone. He never could remember what he said that finally convinced her to agree that they should try to have a child. If only he could have convinced her earlier.

On the sofa, she was already asleep when he spoke

again. Instead, he looked out the window at the night sky and the city lights that kept everything slightly aglow. Katherine's sleeping breaths were steady and constant. A flickering in the distance, vague at first, became more distinct. He knew at once what it was. It had made him gasp the first time he saw it: a house on fire. It was three or four blocks away, entirely engulfed in flames. Wisps of fire reached into the sky. He watched it with enthusiasm as if it were something to be mesmerized by rather than a possible tragedy in the making.

Without being told, he knew the house would be empty, that its inhabitants had just left in order to move south. The fire was there because the house's occupants intentionally set it ablaze. Nine out of every ten house fires across the country were the result of such acts. Maybe the few remaining volunteer firefighters would arrive and put it out so it didn't spread to the neighboring houses. But maybe they wouldn't. It was a guarantee that the police wouldn't take a report. The few remaining cops never bothered investigating house fires anymore because they too understood that the arsonists were on their way south. What were they going to do, extradite them back to Philadelphia just as the city was getting ready to evacuate?

He still didn't understand why it happened. He knew what the people were thinking when they lit the match, but he didn't understand the reasoning that got them to that point. They were doing it because they were leaving the area for good, heading south, and didn't want anybody else to live in the home that held special value for them, as though a family from Montreal or Syracuse would taint their house's memories. It took a special kind of egotism to think a house that was built fifty years earlier, had been lived in by three other families before they had lived in it, held some special significance strong enough for one family and one family only. Good riddance to whoever it was.

The proper thing to do, the custom that people everywhere had taken to as they moved further south, was to leave their house in proper working order for the next people who wanted it. The doors remained unlocked. The garage was left open. Some people even went as far as to vacuum and dust before they left. These were the people who understood they were beginning the next part of their life, and that somebody else was taking part in the same journey as well. These people knew that karma always repaid its debts.

Part of him thought about waking Katherine so she could see the house burning. It was a no-win situation, though. She would be terrified if he woke her up to see another burning home. But if he didn't, if she found out the next day, she would be afraid to fall asleep at all for fear of what happened when she was dreaming. That was just how she worked. The first time he saw one of the fires, she had been brushing her teeth.

"Hey, honey," he had called to her and she appeared in the bathroom doorway. "Check this out."

At the time, neither of them was accustomed to people burning down their houses on their way out of the city. Both of them had thought it was a life or death situation. Like a fool, he had called 911. Ever since then, she had never been able to see one of the house fires without feeling a sense of dread. Each time, she would start packing their bags while he convinced her it was better to leave with everyone else as the entire city—what was left of the city—made the trip to Washington together.

And so he let her sleep. She would see the smoldering remains the next morning, and when that happened he would feign surprise and act like he hadn't seen anything either. It was, he had learned, the best way to handle things. Live and learn.

Hours later, surrounded by boxes of paper once again, he was still thinking about how to keep her from getting upset so often. All around him were cabinets full of paperwork that no longer served a purpose. The boxes behind him contained photocopied records of every single invoice dealing with sustaining the living quarters. Somewhere else on base there were boxes full of similar invoices which detailed the amounts, dates of purchase, and vendor POCs for the dining halls. He had no idea where those boxes were, but they were taking up at least twenty square feet of space somewhere else on Fort Dix. Somewhere else on the base were boxes of paper dealing with every mechanical part of every piece of equipment, every gun, every computer, everything. And those were just the invoices, a tiny blip on the paperwork radar compared to the military's annual reports, its progress reports, the annual inspection results, the yearly performance results. They had reports for everything.

What was the point of it all? How many acres of forest were chopped down just so Jeffrey had a barrier fortress of boxes for when Lieutenant Miller came by with water balloons as part of a surprise attack?

Other officers were resigning their posts and leaving in the middle of the night with their families. From the limited news he heard across the country, the same thing was occurring all throughout the military: a colonel or a major snuck away one night and the remaining lieutenants drew straws to see who would be lucky enough to move from a cubicle to a private office. One by one the lower ranks filtered into the luxurious carpeted offices of former generals until even the lowly sergeants could close their doors and put their feet up on their desks for a post-lunch nap.

There was a time when personnel were categorized as essential or non-essential. Essential personnel had to perform their duties even during the most severe weather emergencies or other unplanned crises. Jeffrey's feelings weren't hurt by the knowledge that there was nothing about his job that could ever be twisted to make it be considered "essential." These days, it was an outdated category anyway; no one was essential anymore. The guard post's practice of checking badges to get on base was no longer enforced. A man in shorts and a t-shirt had walked past his office the previous week. Jeffrey had never seen the man before. The man walked around the base for a while before disappearing. No one had even bothered to detain him and ask who he was or why he was wandering the base.

There was no reason to keep the planes fueled or to continue performing maintenance on them. No one did their morning jogs or push-ups. Marching was completely extinct. No one bothered saluting anyone else. All around the base were men who knew they were only biding their time until they packed up with the rest of the city and moved south.

The schools were already closed. The teachers were either building generators and food processors as part of the Survival Bill or enjoying early retirement. The last students through the high schools' halls had become young adults and were working alongside the previous generation until the Survival Bill's provisions were complete. One of Jeffrey's old math teachers, a seventy year-old man who couldn't stand not working (doing nothing meant you might as well be dead) was working on roads crews to keep the highways patched and functioning. Every day on his way to work Jeffrey passed his old Algebra teacher manning a paving machine and laying fresh blacktop.

The roads were in better shape than the runways. An F-14 trying to take off from the main Fort Dix runway would blow out its tires and skid into a fiery heap before ever getting off the ground. Any planes that still resided on base were destined to remain there for the rest of time.

The constant paving of roads, though, made people feel safe because it kept them reassured that travel was still possible. God help the fear mongering that occurred each time a car's tire went flat because of a pothole. The nightly talk shows put up a picture of a Porsche with a flat tire, as if anyone should be driving a small sports car these days.

What they really needed, Jeffrey thought, was for the road crews to abandon the constant paving and re-paving and focus solely on clearing abandoned cars from the sides of the road. A family of four that owned three cars only needed the largest vehicle for their trip south. The other two cars would be put to better use, the family thought, if they were left with the keys in the ignition on the shoulder of the highway. The only problem with that practice was that abandoned cars started piling up on the freeways. It wasn't long before not only the shoulder of the highway was blocked, but also the far right lane, and then the middle lane. Some nights on his way home from work, traffic was still as slow with only a hundred cars on the road as it had been when there were thousands drowning each lane.

What genius designated a major highway as the dumping ground for fully functioning automobiles? Why not some place where the remaining people weren't inconvenienced, like Fairmount Park? He knew the reason. Everyone did: people were, by their very nature, inconsiderate and selfish. They wanted to feel like they were doing something good by leaving their cars for whoever else needed them, but instead of taking them someplace out of the way, they were in a hurry to get further south and resettle ahead of everyone else. They didn't care that their shitty little car was blocking the middle lane of the goddamn highway, they were just happy to be able to say "Well, that was my good deed of the day!" before driving south and leaving the state forever.

The reserve of available cars, along with the lack of any meaningful police force, also meant there were as many traffic accidents as there had been when the city's population was at one hundred percent, even though only half the city was occupied. With backup cars readily available and no fear of receiving a ticket or getting a higher insurance premium, drivers used their vehicles like bumper cars. One night on his way home from work, Jeffrey saw an old woman side swipe a middle-aged man for no better reason than she didn't feel like using her turn signal. Another time, he saw two drivers caught up in a bout of road rage trying to drive each other off the highway on their way home from work. If any of their cars became damaged too badly, they could just get out and get in any other car they wanted.

Only a month earlier, a black Lamborghini had pulled into the Becksten's driveway across from Jeffrey and Katherine's house. Charlie Becksten got out, saw Jeffrey, and waved to him. The week before he had been driving a white sedan.

"I've always wanted one of these," Becksten called across the street, a dumb grin plastered to his face. "Found it out on 295. Figured I might as well upgrade."

Becksten was the one man dumb enough not to realize the Great De-evolution made the deteriorating roads a nightmare for luxury cars. Jeffrey was sure he would find a white sedan parked in the middle of 295 the next day, sitting in one of the lanes where the black sports car had been previously. Everyone was doing the same thing. Hopper, the lieutenant who worked down the hall from Jeffrey, had shown up to work the week before riding a

Harley Davidson that he had found in an abandoned shopping center.

"Always wanted one of these," the man had said to Jeffrey with a smile so big he had a hard time pronouncing his consonants. It was the happiest Jeffrey had ever seen the other man.

Jeffrey's eyes opened. It was easy to fall asleep these days, even at work. He missed the days when he would get to the base with a list of too many things to get done. Those were the days that would fly by—it would be time to go home to Katherine before he knew it. Now, there was never a day when he actually had to do anything. Not that day, that week, or, really, ever.

Officers were sneaking away one by one. No one was going to care if an Airman First Class reported for duty or not. One day, Jeffrey and five other officers had gone to the supply room and catalogued every piece of clothing that still existed on base, doing so for no better reason than they were bored. The six men spent the day checking off boxes for boots, belts, shirts, and pants, by color, size, and camouflage pattern. It only took them ninety minutes. The rest of the day they stayed in the storage room and took bets on when they thought the base would close down permanently.

One of the men had thrown his hands in the air and said, "Whatever. No one cares about this place anymore." Another man chipped in: "There was a day when every base probably had a Russian spy. You couldn't pay the Russians to care about this place now."

Previously, before the Blocks appeared, the same chore of cataloging gear would have been assigned to one man to supervise and to four others to perform, and would have lasted two weeks. Everything had been so extraordinarily and unnecessarily complex back then.

No one even cared about maintaining the barracks; everyone had vacant houses to choose from. Even people who had been homeless before the Great De-evolution now had a place to call their own. One of the few feel-good stories on the news from the previous month showed a man who had been living on the streets for forty years, now in his sixties, moving into the abandoned mansion of the Eagles' star wide-receiver. Of course, the same station reported three days later that the man burned the mansion to the ground before disappearing in the night. Such was the world.

**

The tank continued north along the beach. He passed signs for places he had heard of but never been to, places like Long Branch, Sea Girt, Spring Lake, Shrewsbury, Avon-by-the-Sea. When he passed a sign for Loch Arbour, he thought back to a girl he had known in college who had grown up there. Sarah was her name. Or Stephanie. Something with an 'S'. It was a long time ago—before he married Katherine, before Galen was born. A different lifetime. The girl, whatever her name had been, had dated Jeffrey's best friend in college until, both of them drunk at a party one night, his roommate punched the girl right on her mouth in front of everyone. Jeffrey had leapt over Katherine's chair and, with one swing, broken his roommate's nose. When news of the fight made its way back to the school administrators, Jeffrey had actually been forced to attend two weeks of anger management classes, proof that the world's priorities had been jumbled even before the Great De-evolution. Jeffrey and his old roommate never spoke again.

At Monmouth Beach he pulled over, filled the tank

with gas, making sure the reserve canisters were also full in case he got stuck too far away from the next functioning gas station. It wasn't until then that he thought about what other supplies he might need. All he had with him were the clothes he was wearing and the tank. He had no toothbrush, no other pairs of pants or t-shirts, no extra socks or underwear. Not even a roll of toilet paper. These were things he was going to need if he was serious about making his own way.

He left the tank outside Granson's Seafood Buffet before wandering away from the main strip to find a hardware store. The place he came across was the size of an ice cream shop, with nothing more technical than hammers and screwdrivers. He took a couple of simple tools, put them in a duffle bag, and looked for whatever else he might need. He took a container of industrial cleaner and some clean rags. Behind the counter he found a stack of blankets and took two of those as well.

A dog was sniffing at the tank's tread when he went back outside. He saw two possible outcomes: either the animal would want his companionship and follow him around, or it would be wild and attack him. But neither of these things happened. When it saw Jeffrey, the dog merely turned, walked away, and disappeared.

He put the tools in the tank before walking in the opposite direction to find personal hygiene supplies. He expected to find someone in the stores he went past, but each one was empty and quiet. Not a single person watched him from a store window or met him in the street. There was a drug store at the end of the next block. Other than the dog, there wasn't a sign of life in the little town.

Compared to the hardware shop, the drug store was picked over. The batteries were all gone. The packs of rubber bands were even gone, although he could think of no reason for someone to have hoarded them. Even the condoms were gone. At least whoever headed south was being responsible. He picked up a tube of toothpaste and a toothbrush. Almost all of the soap was still there. Whoever took the condoms and rubber bands was going to smell like absolute shit, but they would never run out of various forms of rubber. He took a bar of soap. There was only one pack of socks left. He took those as well.

Even though he hadn't seen a single person since leaving Fort Dix, he kept feeling like it was a matter of time until he would see someone else. All he was presented with was barren land without another living person, but he kept expecting the opposite. If there was a man or a family still in one of the towns he had driven through, though, they were keeping to themselves. Tanks were supposed to mean destruction, invasion. An armored machine appearing in town wasn't very inviting compared to a cute little Volkswagen or a convertible.

He wondered if Griggs would tell anyone about the missing tank. What was there to say? It wasn't like they would come north just to reclaim their property. He wondered how the preparations for the drive south were going, and as hard as he tried not to, he wondered what Katherine was doing. She might have gone over to her parents' house after the call with Jeffrey and the disaster at the stadium. What kind of comfort did she think they might be able to provide? When he thought about her getting ready for the trip, he imagined Galen there with her.

He also found himself thinking of all the things he would say to Galen as they passed by each beach town, as if the boy would be there with him the next time he made a similar trip. Sometimes he actually said these things out loud.

"I used to know a girl from there… It looks like it

might rain… For coming out of a freezer, that was a pretty good steak."

Other times, he had a quiet conversation in his head. But always, he was thinking of Galen being there by his side, just like they had been on the porch together all those nights.

After stocking up on supplies, the engine came to life again. The tread began moving. A minute later, he was leaving Monmouth Beach, heading north once more.

Chapter 5

Three more people were missing from Fort Dix when he went in to work on Monday. One was a second lieutenant who had remained in the military over the years even though he got passed up for every possible promotion. Another was the last remaining colonel. The few remaining men all wondered what the point was to showing up anymore. They certainly weren't required to be there, they just kept appearing each day as if it were the only thing they knew to do.

No one in Washington cared if the base was open or not. There were no battles to fight, no borders to protect. There were no secrets worth guarding anymore. The televised meeting of spies had proven that. Jeffrey wasn't sure which rumors coming out of Washington could be trusted and which were make-believe. He imagined a room full of generals bickering over the future of the Pentagon.

One general, much more forward thinking and progressive than the rest, would suggest the entire five-sided superstructure be opened to the public and turned into a Block shelter. The other generals would all laugh.

One of the generals would groan, "Christ, is he serious?"

Another of the men would rub his eyes to show he was running out of patience. "You want to relegate this building, where the Secretary of Defense has led the armed forces through some of our country's most important wars, to nothing more than a nursing home for thousands of Blocks?"

The man saying this wouldn't mention the fact that the acting Secretary of Defense had supposedly loaded a private helicopter with his family, headed south, and would never be heard from again.

Maybe a similar conversation was what had led Washington to open Area 51 to the public. After the fears caused by the Russian spy at the end of the TV special, the goodwill gesture would show people there was nothing to be afraid of. Jeffrey could see how the room full of generals would think it was a good idea: it would give everyone something to take their minds off the fading population. Maybe they finally realized it was a matter of time until the last guards would abandon their posts and every single military installation would go back to nature anyway.

The evening news was happy to have something to talk about other than the end of the world. After the Area 51 announcement was made, the exodus toward the clandestine base was discussed every night.

The people in Reno were so excited to see what secrets were there that they stopped waiting for the Portland community to join them. Two months later, when the people of Portland did finally arrive at Reno, the entire city was already empty. The people of Grand Junction drove straight through Utah without restocking on supplies because they wanted to see what secrets were so incredible the government had to hide them all these years. Even one of Jeffrey's neighbors would leave the neighborhood suddenly because he wanted to see an alien for himself.

The government, thinking it had been doing something nice for the people, something to offer a distraction, didn't realize the effect the news would have on everyone; even people in the cities that would one day become the final southern settlements packed up for spontaneous road trips. A series of vans left Los Angeles to see what was in the Nevada desert. The same thing happened in Houston and Miami, the news giving people a different kind of madness to take their minds off the insanity of a species slowly dying off. At no other time during the Great De-evolution would so many vehicles head north instead of south.

After hearing of legendary expeditions to map the western frontier, of gold rushes out west, of races to the moon, people couldn't resist one last adventure, and they paid for it. Families that had already safely relocated amongst large groups of people found themselves back on the roads again, stuck on the side of the highway with flat tires once more. A group of three minivans became stranded in the middle of Death Valley National Park. All of the passengers died. Countless cars were abandoned on the long, barren stretches of Route 40. Two men, excited to see what was fact and what was fiction, disappeared near Yosemite National Park and were never seen again. A husband and wife and their two Block children all died of dehydration outside Flagstaff when their car broke down and no one else stopped to help. Hundreds of stories cycled through the country. Everyone knew someone who had gone to see what was in Area 51 or had a friend that knew someone who died on the way.

The mysterious base that everyone had seemingly known the location of when it was a secret, suddenly became hard to find. A trio of men took a wrong turn and died on a desert road just outside Caliente, Nevada. A woman, her Block sister sitting idly by in the passenger seat, drove back and forth between Reno and Las Vegas three times before her car finally broke down near a lake with no name. Trapped in the woods surrounding the anonymous lake, the woman was attacked and killed by a bear. Her sister was eaten an hour later by a pack of wolves. A couple from San Diego got stuck on the side of the road and thought it best to attempt the hike straight through Death Valley. Surely, they couldn't have thought they would make it, but memories of old episodes of "The X-Files" drove them forward anyway. Their sun-bleached skeletons would remain in the desert over the final decades, without another person ever setting eyes on them, until even the final settlements eventually died out.

The people who did successfully arrive at the abandoned base faired little better. Most of them had driven the last stretch of road on flat tires. A few were forced to walk the final miles after their car couldn't travel any further. None of them had a way to leave the remote facility once they were there. The base's Humvees had been taken when the last government personnel abandoned the facility. Everybody was stuck there. And for that reason, the super secret Area 51 became an unofficial final settlement, and the first of the final settlements to eventually go quiet when the last person there no longer took another breath.

They did die satisfied, though. Every night, a web cam allowed them to be interviewed on the news about the various things they were finding, all of which had previously needed a Top Secret clearance to see. They told of a hangar full of experimental aircraft. One of the ships, they said, looked like a futuristic car with tiny wings on either side. Another was almost completely flat, a sheet of flying metal, except for a bulb where the pilot would sit. These and all of the other advanced prototypes were completely black, as though a black UFO in the sky would be harder to spot than one which was painted white or blue.

In one of the empty offices, people found schematics for what appeared to be a series of long-range missiles. Another office had documents discussing theoretical equipment to control the weather. A file cabinet had folders containing experiments with mind control.

And then, in the basement of the basement, level 2LL, was a large open room with a green body floating in formaldehyde. The body was not of this earth. Many of the people thought a joke was being played on them because the body looked exactly like the generic space aliens they always saw on cartoons and "Unsolved Mysteries"—large eyes, tiny hands, no hair. After spending their entire lives being sure that something was hidden there, then finding it, they momentarily refused to believe it was real. For these people in the desert, it was proof that Lee Harvey Oswald wasn't the lone shooter, that Bigfoot did exist, that something otherworldly was happening in the Bermuda Triangle. Each night, the stranded Area 51-ers would give another interview on the news, then eat dinner together and talk about what it must have been like for that alien to crash so far away from home. All of them hoped it had died in the wreck so it didn't have to know the types of experiments men would perform on it.

Jeffrey didn't want to think about Area 51 or the generals in the Pentagon, though, because he had his own problems. He was sitting amongst a table of his peers, half of whom suggested they just "get it over with" and close Fort Dix as well. It wasn't serving any purpose to the city, to the country, or to anyone else.

One of the men said, "We can't just close up, can we?"

"That's what they did in Fairchild Air Force Base in Washington. They didn't even tell anybody else they were going to shut the base down. They all agreed amongst themselves and left the Pentagon out of it."

"I heard they did the same thing in Grand Forks," another man said.

Phones still worked. Email still worked. Any one of them could have picked up a phone or sent a message asking what the present condition was at either of those bases or any other base, but they were all content with repeating what they had heard.

One of the men said his wife was sick more often these days than she used to be. The lieutenant colonel didn't have to say he believed the rumors that Blocks might make you sick, but everyone knew that's what he was getting at. It was better left unsaid since half of the men in the room had Block daughters or sons, or had a brother or sister with one.

Corporal Rawicz asked if anyone knew when the relocation to Washington was going to take place. "Can you believe this shit?" the man said. "Don't you think the military should at least be in the loop? If we don't know what's going on, who does?"

Someone else added, "Why can't they make a schedule for everyone? At least that way we would have a weekly countdown instead of always wondering if today will be the day."

The room fell silent. One of the lieutenant colonels farted and the rest snickered. They were boys at heart.

It was an hour later when Jeffrey walked back to his office. No decisions had been made. The group of men, used to being given orders, couldn't make one for themselves. Jeffrey sat at his desk with his feet propped on top of a stack of three boxes. He could close his eyes and go to sleep and no one would bother him the rest of the day.

He wondered why he kept showing up to work when it wasn't necessary. It wasn't for the camaraderie. It wasn't out of a sense of duty. What was it then? He shrugged his shoulders. Times were changing. It would be important to learn how to discard all of the things you used to hold dear that no longer had importance. If he couldn't let them go, they would weigh him down in his new life.

On the television that night, the tall, slender man said, "When asked again today for a relocation date for our city's move to Washington, do you know what our beloved Mayor said? He said he doesn't know! Can you believe that? If the Mayor doesn't know, who does?"

The other man pulled his shirt away from his neck so it didn't suffocate him. "Don't you think the Governor should have something to say about it? The Governor shouldn't be putting our Mayor in this position."

"We didn't elect the Governor to run our city, we elected the Mayor for that job. And, by the way, when was the last time anyone saw the Governor? He might already be in Mexico, for all we know."

Katherine flipped the television off. With the room dark, she turned on her side to face Jeffrey. He could see her outline and a glimmer, a diamond, of glowing light on her eyes. Everything else was invisible.

"Why haven't we talked about what we're going to take with us?" she asked. "It's strange that the move is coming up soon, but we haven't talked about which things we'll take."

Even in private, he hadn't given thought to what was important and what could be left behind. Each time he sat in his office, surrounded by useless boxes, not once did he wonder what the equivalent useless objects were in his house and if he would be upset to leave them behind. There hadn't been a time when he had passed through their bedroom and seen a photograph or a coffee mug or an old tie and thought, *I really want to make sure I take that with me to Washington when the time comes to pack all of our things.*

He didn't want her to feel alarmed: "What would

you like to take? We can take whatever you want."

"We'll take as many changes of clothes as we can fit in three bags. And we'll take our laptop so we can stay in touch with people when we move." She had obviously been thinking about it without him.

He said, "We can scan all of our old photo albums and take a disc. That will save a lot of space. We can have all of our old photos from high school and our wedding on a CD that doesn't take up any room."

Her mouth turned into a pained smile, her cheeks looking like they wanted to assist in the smile but her mouth refusing to curve up at the ends. It was the look she gave when she was suddenly so upset that she might cry.

"You'd be willing to leave the originals here to rot? What if we left them here and some family from Canada moved in and threw the albums in the backyard to get rained or snowed on?"

What will happen, he thought, *when we die? The pictures will end up as trash, either now or later*. But he didn't say anything.

"I'll need to take my mother's jewelry box." She looked at it sitting atop her dresser. "And my grandfather's coin collection."

"Just pack whatever you want," he said. "We'll see how much space we have after we've narrowed it down some."

She squeezed his arms to let him know that answer was to her liking. "Are you going to check in at the Pentagon or Bolling Air Force Base when we get to D.C.?"

She had no idea what Fort Dix was like anymore, but if he told her she would only panic and say they needed to move south right away. More and more, he wasn't sure what he should tell her and what he shouldn't, and because of it he said little or nothing at all.

"If we turn the TV back on, you have to promise we won't watch that damn show. All it does is upset you."

"You aren't worried?" she asked.

"Everything always works out for the best."

Instead of speaking, she scooted closer to him and put her head against his shoulder. When he put his arm around her, she didn't shake or whimper, but thirty years of being married let him know she was crying.

"When I was a little girl I used to think I'd live in the country and take care of horses all day. I'd get up early in the morning, have coffee with my dad, and then the rest of the day I'd be outside combing horses, feeding them, riding them, talking to them. When we first got married I, well, I guess I didn't have an exact course in mind for how things might go, but I was still happy. Now I sit at home and take care of Galen all day."

That wasn't true and they both knew it: Galen didn't need much attention, he barely needed anything at all really. All he needed was a re-filled nutrient bag each day. And an occasional cleaning. Everything else they did—talking to him, giving him companionship, even simple things like brushing his teeth and shaving him—they did just so they could feel like Galen was more a part of their lives than he actually was. Those things offered a window to what it was like to have a regular child, nothing more.

"Every night," she continued, "I get up after you've gone to sleep. I sit at the window and watch which neighbor will leave next."

That wasn't true either, unless, in his old age, he was becoming a sound sleeper. When they were first married he would wake up every time she so much as shifted her weight. On a couple of different occasions he had woken up to find her briefly look out the window on her way to use the bathroom in the middle of the night. Had those actually been times she was staring out the window for hours, only to act like it was in passing once he stirred?

They were surrounded by silence. There was no chance Galen would interrupt them, no chance that a nightmare would wake him up or that he would sneak out of bed to listen to their argument.

It was Katherine who finally said, "What if something happens to you? I'd have to take care of Galen by myself. What if we take him with us on the trip to Washington and something happens then?"

"Don't say 'if we take him.' We're taking him. Don't talk like that." He never raised his voice or said nasty things to her, but her simple choice of words, intentional or not, made him want to yell at her so the few neighbors left on their street could hear that his son was never to be taken for granted, was to be given every consideration that any father would give his son. "Everything will be fine," he said. "Don't worry so much."

"What if we get to Washington and they don't have enough empty houses?"

"People are leaving Washington to go further south just the same way people here are already going to there. It's not just us moving on. Look at how many new faces we see each day. And they never arrive to a lack of vacant homes. Hell, they have twenty houses to choose from in this neighborhood alone. There will be plenty of empty places for us to pick from."

They stayed on the sofa in the same position, in silence, until she was asleep. He wanted to say, "The three of us are going to grow old together. You're going to get mad at me because I'm going to be a cranky eighty-year old man who constantly farts and asks you to repeat yourself." He didn't want to wake her, though, so he said nothing.

She woke a moment later, mumbling about a quick dream in which they had a normal child.

"Who wants a kid who can talk back or break curfew or thinks they know everything just because they're young?"

"Don't say things like that," she said. They stared at each other, both trying to remember the younger version of the person next to them, the person they had fallen in love with so long ago. "I love our son, but don't say we're lucky to have a Block. Don't say that."

And just like that, they were dangerously close to the one argument they could never resolve. She had been three months pregnant the first time she told him they shouldn't have tried having a baby.

"But you wanted one," he had said. And then, before she could say anything: "We both did."

"You said we should do this, not me."

They had both wanted kids at one point. It was just that Katherine didn't want to try once the Blocks appeared. Jeffrey still had.

As a young man he had been dumb enough to say things like, "We wouldn't even be having this conversation if we would have tried having a kid earlier. We should have tried right after getting married, instead of waiting."

The numbers backed him up: the first Blocks weren't identified until Jeffrey and Katherine had been married for five years. But once they had appeared, they outnumbered the regular children three years later, before being the only children born within six years of their first appearance.

She had only agreed to have a child because Jeffrey told her everything would work out for the best. She didn't have to agree to try to have a child, but she wanted to make him happy. He didn't think about all the times she said they should wait until a Block cure was found or all the times he said there was still a small chance of them having a normal baby (this was four years after the Great De-evolution had started). The longer they waited, he would tell her, the more they were pushing their luck.

He cringed these days as he replayed those old arguments. One time he had told her, flat out, that having a Block son was her fault because she was the one who had wanted to wait. As if watching a horror movie, an immature version of himself had tried to make himself feel better by making her feel worse.

"You're right," she had said, her tone letting him know something nasty was going to follow. "Lord knows we were ready to be parents straight out of high school, right? And it made perfect sense to get pregnant before you went off to basic training, right?" She looked at him with narrowed eyes the way a beautiful red fox would just before chasing down a rabbit and ripping its throat apart. She yelled into his face: "Everything would have been just fine if I would have listened to the oh-so-wise lord of the house. Grow up, Jeff." When he didn't say anything she growled and added, "This was a mistake."

She didn't say which part she was referring to that was a mistake, and he didn't ask because there were too many answers he wouldn't like.

"You're the one who wanted a son so badly," she said. "Now you have your precious son and he's not going to be able to talk to you or do anything with you. He's going to sit in bed all day, or in his wheelchair. So there you go."

"Don't talk about my son—our son—like that."

In all their years of marriage, that had been the only time he got so mad at her that he packed a bag and stayed somewhere else for a while. That "somewhere else" ended up being the living room sofa because he couldn't bring himself to actually open the front door and drive away, not even for one night. It might not have been so bad if the sofa had folded out. The joke was on him: he still remembered the conversation with Katherine years earlier when they were shopping for new furniture and she suggested they buy a sofa that folded out in case they had guests over. He had said it wouldn't be necessary.

Two days later they had made up and he was sleeping in the same bed again.

Before Galen was born, they had talked about their hopes for their child. Of course they had both wanted the baby to be normal, the difference was that Katherine had never failed to let it be known how crushed she would be if it wasn't regular, while Jeffrey always made sure to say he would love any child he was given. Katherine had wanted someone she could see off to the school bus each morning, a child who cleared the table after dinner, someone who would eventually fall in love and let Katherine become a grandmother.

While Katherine's belly got bigger and bigger, the ratio of regular babies diminished, replaced by Block babies. The chances their son would come out crying also diminished. As the ninth month approached, Blocks made up ninety-five percent of newborns. Katherine was constantly throwing up then. Things she said made Jeffrey think she was making herself sick from obsessing about the possibility of a near comatose baby growing inside her. To her, it might as well be a still-born child growing in her womb all those months. He would lie in bed and hold her as she begged for the baby to kick just once, just one time. Through it all, Jeffrey told her everything would be fine. Things always worked out for the best.

During check-ups, they had refused to let the doctor tell them the fate of their child; they wanted to be surprised when Galen was born. They knew it was going to be a boy, that much of the surprise was OK if it was ruined ahead of time, but they both agreed they didn't want to know whether Galen would be born a Block until they actually laid eyes on him.

His birth should have brought tears of joy and yells of celebration, but Katherine burst out crying when the baby refused to make a sound. She held it in her arms like a doll.

"Stop that," Jeffrey had snapped. He didn't care that her parents were staring at him. He never settled on whether or not they had been staring in shock at a man who would yell at his wife right after giving birth, or in admiration at a father who would protect his son from insult. Or maybe they were simply staring at a Block baby for the first time, amazed at how close it was to a real baby, yet completely silent, completely still.

"I knew we shouldn't have risked it," she had said when they got home from the hospital. The single sentence had been enough. She might as well have said, "Why did you force me to get pregnant against my will? I didn't want any of this and now look what happened. I hope you're happy with your mute and motionless son. We should name him Burden."

He thought back to the hospital's nursery and how he hadn't even realized what it was at first because there were no crying babies. The room contained eight children, all of whom had been born within the past week. None of them were begging to be picked up. None of them were crying to be fed. It was an amazing thing to see. It was more like a room full of Hollywood props than it was a real room with real, breathing newborns. And they would be that way for the rest of their lives.

He had tip-toed up the aisle, knowing all the while that being quiet wasn't necessary, until he spotted a sticker with his son's name scribbled on it. The baby's stillness, its perfect calm and quiet, made Jeffrey instantly protective. Maybe he would have been anyway, but seeing how defenseless his little boy was turned him into a lion. Something about the child not being able to call out if it needed help made him want to be there more than if the child was wailing for milk. He cried then, not because his son would never talk or move or do anything a normal son would do, but because the life his finger tips were touching—yes, there was a beating heart and blood flowing through those veins—was his very own son. His son.

All he said was, "You're my boy. I'll always protect you."

That night, as Jeffrey held Galen in his arms, he had told the child, "You're the lucky one. You won't have to go through the misery of being around mean kids or having your heart broken by a girl. You'll never have to sit at a job you don't like just so you can support your family."

It was the first of many times over the years that he would say the same thing as he watched Galen grow from an infant, to a teenager, and then to a young adult, all the while sitting still and not uttering a single sound.

When Jeffrey had a bad day at work he went to Galen's room and said, "You're so lucky you'll never have to put up with bosses that don't know anything." When he got home late he said, “You’re so lucky you’ll never have to sit in rush-hour traffic.” When the politicians still couldn’t agree on anything, even as the human population started decreasing for the first time in history, he told Galen, “You’re so lucky you don’t have these bastards speaking on your behalf. If it was up to them, no one would ever make a decision.” There was always a reason to tell Galen that he was the lucky one in the family.

Just saying the words, giving his fears and his ambitions credence, helped. Maybe if Katherine sat down with Galen more often and had the same kind of talks she wouldn’t be so negative. Or maybe when she spoke to Galen, she would focus on the things that bothered her each day. Maybe talking to a Block was like talking to a reflection of yourself and whatever you had to offer to the world was what you got back.

But instead of talking to Galen when she had the chance, she remained quiet. The times she did sit in a room with him and Jeffrey happened to be walking past the doorway, he saw her staring at the boy’s face or out the window. She was always thinking about something, always remembering a thought from the past or lost in daydreams.

Years later, after many iterations of the argument, she had asked Jeffrey why he spent so much time sitting on the porch talking to Galen, as though talking to his son was a waste of time that could be better spent cleaning dishes or working on the yard, something that would make their lives easier, or at least something with a measurable benefit.

He had turned to her and answered her question with his own: “Why don’t you spend more time talking to him?” A variation of the same Galen argument started up again that time too.

“Our words fall on deaf ears.” She gave a dry laugh at her black humor.

"God damn it, don't make fun of our son like that."

There was a ground swell of resentment in those years, as the very last normal babies were being born, against parents who insisted on trying to have a child anyway. It bothered Jeffrey when neighbors or co-workers would later ask round-about questions to find out when Galen was born, as though he and Katherine got what they deserved because they waited as late as they had. It didn't bother him that other people wanted a reason to feel superior to him; it bothered him because Katherine would sometimes accept the guilt they wanted to place on her as she lied about Galen's age. She would say Galen was a couple of years older than he actually had been so that when the other couples did the math in their heads, there was no blame to pass on, only sympathy.

When they got home she would tell him, "Don't you see? Everyone is wondering why we would try to have a kid when there was almost no chance he would be regular? I still don't know how you convinced me."

That part sent him storming out of the house so he didn't yell at her. The argument didn't end there, however. It followed them like an army of termites, hiding behind walls, hiding in dark cracks where it looked like nothing existed, always there, always eating away bit by bit. Sometimes they had the argument twice in one month. Then, as though they had finally exterminated it, it would go away for two years. It always found ways to sneak out again, though.

That night in bed, as the argument became an old memory and everything surrounding them in the room reminded them that they were a married couple of thirty years, they again said they were sorry, both saying they loved the other. If they couldn't help having the argument, they could at least finish it on a civil note.

Jeffrey looked over at the clock and then smiled. “This is the latest we’ve been up in a long time.”

“When we were first dating, we used to stay up this late all the time. Do you know how mad my father used to get when I’d come home late? You’re going to be exhausted for work tomorrow morning.”

“Who cares? Let’s stay up all night.”

She giggled a little, then kissed him.

And they did stay up all night. They talked about the types of people they had been when they were young and dumb. They talked about how they were the only couple they knew who had stayed together after high school, made it through college, and gotten married. All of the other couples had seemed so intent on spending the rest of their lives together too, but they all fell apart the way young romance is bound to do.

“We must have done something right,” she said.

Jeffrey kissed her forehead, then her mouth. “I don’t know how you’ve put up with me all these years.”

They talked about the vacations they had gone on in the years prior to Galen being born. There was the honeymoon to Tunisia, the vacation with her sister and her sister’s husband to the Caribbean, the backpacking trip to hike part of the Oregon trail. Eventually, they got so sleepy that it was tough to keep their eyes open.

The last thought Jeffrey had as he fell asleep was that everything was going to be fine Nothing could defeat them. Not a dwindling city. Not the lost hope of grandchildren. Not the unknown. Definitely not a couple of guys spouting fear on TV. Everything really would be OK. And then he fell asleep.

**

Whenever there was a possible fork in his path, he stayed to the right, close to the sand and the water. The roads were mostly intact, but in some parts they had already deteriorated enough that only the tank would have been able to pass through town; even an SUV would break an axle or have a tire shred apart.

Just outside Keyport he came to a crevice in the road, the size of a swimming pool. The tank dipped into the road until the turret scraped earth as the machine tilted downwards. If the hole were any larger, even the tank would have become stuck. It was easy for a man in a tank to feel invincible, but that one moment was enough for Jeffrey to stop taking his machine for granted. If he abused the capability the tank offered, recklessly putting it in a situation to get stuck, he wouldn't have any other way to keep traveling, except by foot.

The roads, as a whole, were what he expected after the stories he had heard from people coming down from the north. There were some sections of land that didn't seem so bad, but then he drove over other parts that gave credence to the fear-mongers saying the caravan from Philadelphia to Washington would never make it.

It seemed like it should be a simple thing to get a line of vehicles from one point to another. General Patton was able to move thousands of vehicles against an entire army. But times were different. A car would, inevitably, break down, a road would be blocked, people would start crying, Blocks had to be fed and changed. You couldn't very well pull up next to these people and scream at them that they had better follow orders or the Germans would be victorious.

Giant holes in the ground and the constant broken roads along the beach made Jeffrey switch over to the Garden State Parkway. It was in better condition, but was also littered with abandoned cars everywhere. The tank was continually swerving left and right to avoid cars scattered about like marbles.

In a little town called Keasby, he saw a single ribbon of smoke drifting up into the sky. The inferno at the stadium made this tiny string of grey seem trivial. The smoke's source, whether it was a family with a fire going to stay warm, a grill to prepare dinner in the backyard, the remnants of a house burning to the ground, could not be seen. He sped the tank up to get past the smoke. Every time he saw something unique, no matter what it was, he imagined Galen being there with him so his son could see it too. But this time, seeing the smoke, he didn't want to think of his boy.

The first parts of 95 he saw looked like a war zone; the tank fit in nicely. He was only on the highway for a mile before a small caravan of vehicles approached from the north. The line of cars was led by two monster trucks, their wheels as tall as the tank, a body that was jacked up so high the driver needed a ladder to get up and down. Behind the pair of giant trucks was a line of SUVs, the biggest of which looked like a toy compared to the trucks. The main section of vehicles only numbered about thirty. Another ten or so trailed further behind. Jeffrey kept the tank to the side of the road so he wasn't in their way. As they passed by him, he saw each driver and all of the passengers staring at the tank in confusion. None of them slowed down, though, to ask why a tank was heading north. None of them offered as much as a wave or a smile.

Only the very last car in the procession pulled over to the side of the road. A middle-aged man rolled his window down and stuck his head out.

"I have more than one hundred gold bars in my trunk," the man said. "I'll give you half of them in exchange for the tank."

"What do the gold bars do for me?" Jeffrey asked.

The man looked stunned. "Each bar is one hundred ounces of gold. And you'd have over fifty of them. Do you know how much that's worth?"

"What does it do for me, though?" Jeffrey said, staring intently at the man.

"Fine, you can have all one hundred bars."

"What do you think I'll do with it?"

The man looked at the other SUVs beginning to get away from him, then looked once more at the tank. "Screw yourself," the man yelled before giving Jeffrey the middle finger and speeding ahead to join the rest of the caravan.

A couple of minutes after the first procession was gone, the second part approached. This group had no monster trucks or SUVs, but consisted of sedans and mini-vans. This next batch of cars zigged and zagged back and forth across the highway, following the lead car's path to avoid the major potholes. Some of the vehicles were driving on flat tires, the rubber flapping against the ground. It was a matter of time until the tire tore completely off and it was bare metal on concrete. It would be soon after that when the car wouldn't be able to go further anymore. And by that time the monster trucks and the SUVs would be out of sight and gone.

Unlike the first group, the passengers in these cars stuck their heads out the open windows and stared at the tank as though it were an omen meant to bring them safety. Some of the people waved at him until they saw the tank was continuing past them in the opposite direction without stopping. The friendly waves turned to pleas for help.

One man yelled, “Where are you going?” Another screamed, “Please stop. Please help us.”

But the tank kept going.

Twenty minutes later, between Jersey City and Elizabeth, only two miles in actual traveling distance, Jeffrey came upon a single car broken down on the side of the road. The tags said it was from New York. The front bumper was resting on the ground. Both of the driver’s side tires were flat. The back wheel looked like it might be too bent to put on a spare. Behind the car, connected to its bumper, was a small trailer with luggage and spare tires. A man was standing next to the car, his golden retriever at his side. The man had his hands on top of his head as if pleasantly amused to see a tank roaming around.

Jeffrey thought about his parents and how easy their trip south had been years earlier. This was before the Great De-evolution and the first signs that no new children would grow up to think, create, provide. They had merely stepped on a plane and flown down. Their furniture, their belongings, arrived in a truck three days later. Their story seemed magical now.

Instead of people flying south, planes crashed before they could ever take off, the runways unfit anymore for the giant machines. Instead of people taking cruise liners for a tour of the Caribbean, random men with no sailing experience stole whatever boats they could find, and either ended up back on shore ten minutes later or else they drifted into the middle of the ocean until their urine was brown and they were drinking ocean water as a last resort.

The man said something to his dog which Jeffrey couldn’t hear, then he let out a relieved sigh upon seeing that Jeffrey was wearing khakis and a t-shirt instead of fatigues or gang clothes, was smiling instead of yelling demands.

"Hello," Jeffrey said softly, as though his voice might have forgotten how to work.

"Thank you for coming back and getting me," the man said. "We owe you one."

"I'm not with the people you were traveling with," Jeffrey said. Hadn't the man noticed there was no tank in the procession? "No one is coming back from your group. They're gone."

The man looked for the tail end of the caravan, but it was no longer in sight. "Who are you with, then?"

"I'm by myself."

"I'm sure we can catch up to them," the man said. As if on cue, the dog gave a friendly bark.

"I'm going that way," Jeffrey said, pointing north.

The other man frowned. "Why are you heading that way? Are you on a special mission?"

You couldn't very well blame the man—why else would someone with a tank be driving north unless it was part of some covert orders?

"My only special mission is seeing if I can help you. Then I'm back on my way."

"Are you sure you aren't with our group?"

"I'm sure."

"Are you sure you don't want to join our group?"

"I'm sure."

There was no point to carrying on that type of conversation. Neither of them would leave feeling any better.

"Where are you coming from?" Jeffrey asked.

"Near Norwalk. About thirty miles outside New York City."

The man was worse off than Jeffrey first thought. At least let him be from Syracuse and have made tangible progress. He asked how long the man had been traveling.

"Two days." Then, as if it needed explaining, "The roads are rough. But I'm sure someone will come back for us when they notice we're missing."

It was only then that Jeffrey noticed a second figure, motionless, still sitting in the car.

"My daughter," the man said.

As his eyes adjusted to the sunlight, Jeffrey could see flies all over his daughter's face, buzzing every which way. A shudder ran through him. Then the smell hit him. Rotting skin. Feces.

"Jesus Christ," Jeffrey said, taking a step backwards.

"I know what you must think, but it's not like that. I'm not crazy or anything. I know she must not look too good right now. She passed away right before we left for this drive. But I promised my wife she would get to see our daughter again. I promised her."

"Where's your wife?" He had no idea why he was asking.

"She's already in Baltimore. She's waiting for us there. Once I get there, we'll bury Lorrie. But I can't bury her until my wife gets to see her again. I promised."

"You'll never make it."

"But we have to. I promised my wife."

Jeffrey walked to the trailer behind the man's car, took the spare tire off the cart and dropped it next to the flat.

"Listen, we can try to swap out a tire, but I'm not sure it'll go on. The wheels are bent pretty bad. Even if you do get going again, you won't make it far. I'd suggest you take the next exit and settle down at the first place you find."

"Don't bother changing the tire," the man said. "I appreciate the help, but two tires are flat and I only have one spare left. But don't worry, someone will come back for me, I'm sure."

"You can't just sit here and wait. You'll be waiting till you die."

"But we can't leave our group." The man rubbed his dog behind the ear while he spoke. "If we leave the road, they won't be able to find us. And Lorrie needs to see her mom again."

"Your group is already gone. You won't see them again."

"I'm sure they'll send someone back for us," the man said.

The dog did not offer an agreeable bark this time.

"Why would you want to go with them anyway?"

"They said on the radio that everyone in Philly was getting ready to head south to Washington. I figured I would go with them as far as Baltimore and then meet up with my wife." The man looked off in the distance again. "I just don't want to get left behind."

That was exactly what had happened, though. But

instead of being left behind in the comfort of his own home, the man was stuck on the side of the road, in the middle of what used to be a congested highway where truckers battled with commuters to see who could get road rage first.

"Didn't you hear about the fire?"

"We did," the man said, "but it's just the three of us." The dog panted happily upon being included.

"What if they loaded your dog in a stadium and burned it to the ground?"

"Why would they do that to a dog?"

"Why would they do it to Blocks?"

The man didn't offer a response. Jeffrey rubbed the dog behind its ear while the man continued to scan the horizon for a sign of vehicles returning to get him.

"Do you mind if I ask you a question?" the man said. "Why are you leaving? Heading north, I mean."

The sky to the south was still dark. Jeffrey needed to see the plague of ashen clouds to remind himself what had happened there. The dark sky was Jeffrey's answer for the man. His boy wasn't at home with Katherine but had been burned alive next to thousands of other silent people. The last thing his son had ever seen wasn't his father's face, but a stranger's.

"Your friends have abandoned you. You shouldn't try to join them. You won't make it, and you already have everything you need. There are houses just off the highway with food processors and power generators. You'll have a nice yard where you can give your daughter a proper burial. That's all you need. Call your wife. She'll understand."

But the man continued to stare down the highway, waiting for a van or a monster truck to come back.

Jeffrey could swear there were so many flies gathered inside the man's car, collected all over his daughter's face and arms, that he could actually hear their buzzing above the hum of the tank.

"You can do anything you want," Jeffrey said. "But you'll be waiting here the rest of your life. Your daughter is just sitting there. Give her some peace. You could find a nice house and live in quiet."

The man was still staring south. The dog whined as if wanting its owner to shift his attention to anything else but the road. There was no point in Jeffrey waiting with the man any longer. He shook the man's hand, patted the dog one last time, and climbed back inside the tank.

Even if the man did somehow manage to catch back up to the group, he would just be abandoned again a day or a week later. Surely, he had to realize that. Jeffrey liked to imagine the man living out his days with his dog in an abandoned mansion, just the two of them, living without any worries, a nice marker in the backyard for his daughter.

More likely, the man would wait patiently on the side of the road, night after night, next to his broken down car and his decomposing child. His dog would be there by his side, waiting for someone to come back, even though no one would. They would remain there until the man starved to death or an animal got him. And then he would begin to rot next to his daughter. Maybe then, at last, the dog would have enough sense to wander off, get food for itself, and make a new life.

As the tank rumbled up 95 toward New York City, Jeffrey wondered how a man could refuse to see what was happening. How could a man let himself die by the roadside out of blind faith that someone would value his well-being above their own? Why couldn't he see the tragedy of what was unfolding? Was it because it was too painful, or was it because holding onto hope and dying was better than living if it meant you were forced to see the world for what it was?

The poor bastard was going to let himself die on the roadside just because he didn't want to admit he was alone. His daughter, who had never hurt another living thing, would be eaten by bugs in front of him until she was a skeleton. If that was how he was going to be, the man should have taken Galen's spot in the stadium. At least then Jeffrey would have his son, and the dog wouldn't feel forced, out of blind loyalty, to sit on the highway next to its master until the end finally did come.

Chapter 6

"Wake up," Katherine said, her head still resting on the pillow next to his. "You're going to be late for work."

When Jeffrey opened his eyes, the sun was already welcoming him. It never stopped shocking him that a world existed in which the black of night gave way to the brightest mornings one could imagine; nature was amazing for working in such a perfect way. Each day had the potential to be a new start to a new life. Birds were even chirping.

The alarm clock said it was ten o'clock. He couldn't remember the last time he had woken up so late.

"Don't worry about it," he said, pulling her closer. "I'll go in tomorrow and everything will be fine."

He could just as easily never show up to work again and it wouldn't make a difference. Better not to say those things, though. Those comments made alarms go off in Katherine's head. Any reminders that life as she knew it was now coming to an end still panicked her. That was why he didn't add, "Hell, there's no one to write me up. Double hell, I don't even think it's possible to get written up. Triple hell, I don't even get paid, so they can't really reprimand me, let alone discharge me."

"You're not even going to call just to be polite?"

The high school version of himself would have had to spray paint a billboard to get this kind of a worried reaction from her. He wasn't sure whether it was an insult or a compliment that as a middle-aged man, simply not calling out of work warranted the same concern.

If he really wanted to disturb her, he could tell her that he didn't even know who his current boss was anymore after his last boss, a wrinkly-faced commander named Gibson, didn't come into work and would be, like the rest, never heard from again. Commander Gibson had been Jeffrey's third new boss in as many weeks.

In Malmstrom Air Force Base in Montana, with no other generals or even lieutenants left, a squadron of F-22s were loaded with fuel and missiles, for no other reason than the partying pilots wanted to see how much damage they could inflict on a single mountain. The men had nothing better to do with their time. Within a week, a video of the mountain assault had over a million YouTube views. And the only supposed reprimand they got came directly from the Pentagon. All it said was, "Please don't do that again." What else could Washington do? They weren't very well going to send a battalion of men across the country just to arrest some pilots who weren't hurting anyone but themselves (the only fatality came when one of the planes, its pilot too drunk to land properly, crashed in a ball of fire).

Shortly after the target practice on the mountain, all of the men involved had also disappeared. It was rumored the military had in fact sent an assassin to dispose of the pilots in order to keep them from further embarrassing the country. Other people said the massive series of explosions on the mountain uncased an old treasure that had once been featured on "Unsolved Mysteries". The men had disappeared to South America with thousands of pounds of gold and diamonds. Others whispered that the men realized their treasure, which would have been worth hundreds of millions of dollars at one time, was now virtually worthless, and they all went crazy. Still other people said there had never been any gold or any assassin. The men simply blew up a mountain and then went south to Texas to live out the rest of their lives.

At Fort Dix, the only mischievousness had come in the form of the men using General Warrington's portrait as the official latrine for a day. These were the types of things he didn't tell Katherine. If she knew there was no chain of command at a popular military installation, it would just reinforce her notion that she should panic. If he told her there was a hangar full of jets that no one bothered guarding anymore, she would run into the streets yelling as loud as she could. If he told her there were nukes all along the east coast that no one cared to guard, she would go stark-raving mad.

"Now," he said, wrapping her up in his arms, "the important question is what are we going to do together today?"

She smiled and said she would think of possible activities while she made breakfast and he checked on Galen.

Because a nutrient bag kept his son healthy, the boy never had to eat and thus, never had a need for healthy molars and incisors. Even so, the thought of Galen's teeth rotting and falling out made him sick to his stomach. This was why he brushed his son's teeth every morning.

He had even broached the subject one time with Katherine of whether or not they should take Galen to the orthodontist to get braces. She had laughed him out of the room, one of the few times she didn't try to hide that she was laughing at him instead of with him.

It would have helped his cause if she had seen the same TV program that he had watched about how much some of the parents of Blocks were willing to do for their children. Some took their kids to get their haircut in ridiculously expensive salons. Some took their Block children to spas for pedicures and facials. In the south, it was popular for parents to take their Blocks to Cub Scout and Brownie meetings so they could be around other happy, laughing kids, even if their own kids sat quietly in the corner.

A small stack of chocolate pancakes was waiting for him when he got back to the kitchen. He wheeled Galen in between the chairs where he and Katherine would be sitting.

"I was thinking we could drive out to the beach," she said. "Or we could go to the park and have a picnic."

In their high school years, they had made sure to go to Fairmont Park every autumn. In the middle of the park, red, orange, and yellow leaves covered everything. Back in those days, they had actually needed to search out empty spots in the park. Every acre of land was packed with a hundred different couples all with the same idea.

When they went on this day, theirs was the only car in the entire parking lot. Not even a maintenance van or a park vehicle could be found. A series of bikes was leaning against a bike post, all old and rusted, some missing tires or seats. Why should anyone want one when there were abandoned cars lining both sides of the highway?

Not even the homeless, Philadelphia's forgotten, lived in the park anymore. When he got back from being stationed overseas, the park's homeless population had seemingly taken over the public land. The vagrants weren't there now because they had moved into the mansions and luxury townhouses left abandoned after the filthy rich decided to get a head start on the migration south.

Instead of going deep into the park, he put their blankets under the first tree offering shade. Remaining close to the car meant less distance to transport Galen when they were done. Katherine carried the sandwiches and drinks while Jeffrey wheeled their son across the tall grass.

A collection of squirrels formed around them immediately. The critters kept sneaking up to the edge of their blankets like birds poaching breadcrumbs. Katherine counted how many of the little animals were at a tree further down the park, then multiplied that by what she guessed the total number of trees in the park might be.

"Well, that can't be right," she said, frowning. "I came up with about twelve thousand squirrels."

But it may have been close. Ten squirrels were on top of their car, surveying the terrain. Another one was nibbling on the end of Jeffrey's shoelaces. Katherine gasped—a squirrel was in Galen's lap, looking up at the boy's face. Without thinking, Jeffrey lunged for it, but it darted away before he could get it.

Katherine spent her time under the tree re-telling stories of their earlier visits to the park. They had once lost a Frisbee in the top limb of a tree and Jeffrey, in his younger years, had been too stubborn to believe he couldn't climb up and get it back. She reminded him of the time a policeman warned them not to get too friendly with each other back when all they did was make out.

A faint smell drifted toward them from the trees. It wasn't pleasant. Once they noticed it, though, it became impossible to ignore. The smell, like smoke, clung to their clothes and their hair.

He left Katherine to fold the blankets while he investigated the stench. It didn't take him long to find the source. Only twenty yards into the tree line, a blanket of white replaced the normal green and brown ground. It covered an area big enough to lay his house on top of. His first thought was that an entire section of ground must have been spray-painted. But why? It would have gone down in history as the single most senseless act of vandalism in the history of the world.

But when his eyes re-adjusted to the reduced light under the trees, he noticed it wasn't spray paint at all. It was bird shit. Hundreds of pounds, maybe a ton, of bird shit. Not a single blade of grass could be seen under it. His search for its source was as simple as looking up. Above him, returning his stare, were hundreds of owls. Every branch was covered with the slow-blinking creatures. His very first thought—his survival instincts kicking in—was whether owls hunted in packs. He could handle one owl, only sustaining minor cuts, but if they worked as a team he wouldn't make it back to his car. Katherine would be left to wonder why her husband disappeared one day, vanishing into thin air at the park.

He heard a little squeak next to him. A squirrel. The next sound he heard reminded him of the air slipping out from a new jar of peanut butter. One of the owls, its wings making a whooshing noise, flew past Jeffrey's face, scooped up the screaming squirrel, and took it back to the top of the tree. Once it was safely back to its nest, the owl crushed the life out of the little creature with its talons. The other owls all looked extremely excited. The successful hunt, the sound of crunching bones, was driving them insane. Each bird tittered under the cover of leaves. Their wings began twitching. They made eager squawks.

Without taking his eyes off the army of birds, Jeffrey started walking backwards, retracing his steps to where the picnic had taken place. With dogs, you were supposed to walk away slowly. Running would make them dash after you. Was the same true of owls? He had no idea. Each time he took a step backwards he expected a thousand wings to launch themselves at him. But the owls only stared at him as he left.

Galen was waiting to be lifted into the wheelchair and taken back to the car.

"Come on, let's go," he said to Katherine. Looking behind him at the trees, he was already closing Galen's passenger door and walking to his own door.

As their car exited the park, hundreds of owls took flight, ready to annihilate just as many squirrels. The mound of bird crap would get larger and larger until it crept up the side of each tree or spread further across the land. A million years from now every acre of Fairmont Park would be covered in white. Fuzzy tails scattered next to little twig-like carcasses, the only reminder that the squirrels had been there at all.

The day ended the same way it started: with the three of them at the table. Jeffrey and Katherine ate shrimp pasta while a nutrient bag dripped into Galen's arm to keep him healthy. When dinner was over and the plates were in the dishwasher, Jeffrey took his son outside so they could sit on the porch and watch the sun set.

Once there, he recounted the entire day to Galen as if the boy would have forgotten it already. "Everyone else can go their own way and do their own thing. As long as the three of us stick together, we'll get through this."

It made him sad when he realized he could say these things to his Block son but not to his wife. Not sharing his belief that love and hope and good feelings won out in the end just because you wanted them to, she would snort and laugh. Life, she would say, wasn't that pretty and perfect. She was too practical for that. What they needed, she had told him, was to be among an entire city, to be a part of a congregation of people all struggling for the same thing, to know that everywhere she looked people were worried about the same things she was concerned about.

Every once in a while he could hear a baseball hitting an aluminum bat. At the end of their neighborhood, some of the younger men were reliving their days of playing high school baseball. There were no leagues anymore, not even for fun, but a few guys still got together to play once a week after their Block children were in bed for the evening.

Katherine told him he should join them one night.

"I would if Galen could play too," he told her. "I'd be there all the time then."

He never did go down the street and join in one of the games. It would be nice to swing a bat again, to feel it make contact with the ball. But it wasn't nicer than spending time on the porch with his son. Nothing could beat that. He hoped, somehow, his son could know that was how he felt.

**

At the intersection of 95 and Interstate 1, he had the option of going west into Newark, or even further, to the mountains and the reservations. Or he could go east, past Jersey City into New York City. He paused to look at the abandoned cities surrounding him. New York, the great city, looked like it could have been abandoned for a century already.

The skyscrapers, once part of the greatest skyline in the world, were scabbed over with cracked windows or no windows at all. If water and ice could chisel away a little more of the Grand Canyon each year, the man-made structures didn't stand a chance. Without people to maintain the roofs, water leaked into the walls, windows, and floors. It had only taken one bad winter for the ice and water to sneak inside each building. Instead of men and women in business suits, the lobbies were filled with ankle-high standing water, birds flying about, and rats searching for their next meal.

The highway into New York had a billboard for *The Phantom of the Opera* that was faded and yellow, the words barely legible. Another billboard advertised the musical production of Steinbecker's *Mapping the Great De-evolution*, the nonfiction bestseller charting mankind's gradual decline in population. Steinbecker had meant his analysis of the end of the world to be informative, not entertaining, a fact that was apparently lost on the show's producers. Audiences were greeted by a full cast of singers belting out songs with lines like:

In the second decade of the decline,
We're gonna close the schools,
We're gonna close the schools,
We're gonna close those schoolbooks one last time.

In the third decade of our expiration,
We're gonna stop travelling,
We're gonna stop travelling,
We're gonna stop using transportation.

The show's producers had to keep audiences from burning the theatre down. It was, understandably, the last new show to hit Broadway before the lights went off and everyone exited stage left one final time.

Wall Street was also boarded up, the last bells having rung ten years earlier when everyone realized there wasn't a single company that held any intrinsic value. Stacks of paper, noting various stocks of Fortune 500 companies, were either worthless or being traded for pennies on the dollar. What was the point of it? Even the greediest of traders realized each stock would be worth even less the next day and the day after that. Maybe a nickel for two shares of an oil company. Maybe a dime for a hundred shares of a cable company. A week later you could buy the same amount of stock for a penny.

LaGuardia runways looked like they had been bombed by enemy planes. A little crack in the concrete path, usually easy to patch, was two feet wide after just one winter. Two cracks kept spreading until they joined and the ground in between crumbled into a gravel pit.

Central Park, it was rumored, wasn't safe for humans anymore. People said the wolves and coyotes there were killing everything they saw. A half marathon had been organized right before the city was abandoned for Philadelphia. The race was halted, however, as soon as the first pack of runners entered the tree line, were grabbed by wolves, and eaten alive.

Each joint of the Statue of Liberty was tearing apart. The idea that the statue could have somehow lasted hundreds of years into the future, just to be a symbol of man's enslavement to a planet of apes, was preposterous—unless the apes spent part of their time keeping the copper body and iron screws maintained, which seemed even more outlandish. Already, one great arm was lying on the ground and the other was getting ready to fall. The torch was completely gone. He had heard a rumor that a crazed politician couldn't stand the idea of it rotting away after the city was abandoned and had paid for the giant torch to be trucked down to his luxury home in Texas.

A soccer field still had two goals and the feint outline of where games had once been played, but the entire playing surface was now covered in a swamp of weeds.

As much as he tried to remember the city as a place where baseball games had been played, fireworks had exploded over the water, the famous ball had dropped each year, he could only see it for what it was now. He tried to remember being amazed by the lights and the hordes of people the first time he visited the city on a 3rd grade field trip. That trip, so long ago, didn't seem like a part of this life anymore, though.

He had never had a chance to bring Galen to the city. He kept meaning to, year after year, but never did. As he watched the crumbled remains, he wondered what he had done with the time that could have been better spent bringing his son here.

Maybe, he thought, if he had been a better father, Galen would still be around. A better father would have been at his son's side when that last rally was announced instead of sitting at a meaningless job. If he had been a better husband, Katherine wouldn't have felt her only resort was taking their son to a stadium of protesters.

He spent the night just north of the city. It was the first night on his trip spent sleeping inside the tank. He did so, not because he was afraid the animals would get him if he camped under the stars, but because sleeping under the constellations kept him thinking of Galen. The nights he had tried sleeping outside, by the road, he became incredibly lonely, shaking with sadness when he should have been slipping off to dreams. After two nights of this, he realized it was because lying on the ground, under the stars, reminded him of the nights he had spent with Galen, camping in their tiny backyard.

The inside of the tank didn't have any associations that reminded him of time spent with his boy. A sleeping bag, the sounds of crickets, these were things that kept him wishing his son could be there with him. And so he slept inside the metal confines of his cave.

If only he hadn't let Galen out of his sight. That was what dominated his thoughts. He was the boy's father. Father's are supposed to protect their sons, not leave them alone. If only he could have convinced Katherine that everything would be all right.

Asleep inside the tank, it wasn't daylight that woke him up the next morning. It was the heat; he was cooking inside the tank. He was sweating before he knew where he was. He needed two blankets to stay warm at night, but during the day he was drenched in sweat as the sun beat down on the metal.

In the first abandoned home he came across, he used the food processor to make a handful of peanut butter and jelly sandwiches. While there, he realized he hadn't called his parents to let them know he was OK. Surely they would have seen the news and called his house right away. Maybe Katherine had been there and they had spoken to her. What could she say to them? Knowing her, she would refuse to answer the phone so she didn't have to say anything at all.

On a computer at the abandoned house, he read a blog that said the Philadelphia caravan left for Washington the day after the stadium fire. A series of pictures showed the flames and smoke followed by pictures of the destruction afterward. It was one thing to look at the remains of Pompeii. That was distant and unknown to his current life. It was quite another thing to see a horror and know someone you loved, someone special to you, someone who you knew every single thing about, was part of what remained in the charred destruction. Seeing the pictures made him want to kill the next Block protester he came across.

The website said that the Philadelphians, after two days of travel, had only made it twenty miles toward Washington. There had been more abandoned cars blocking the highways than previously estimated. There was talk, supposedly, that representatives from the capital would travel out to meet the Philadelphians and tell them to go back home.

Who could blame the people in Washington for wanting the Pennsylvanians to turn back? Rumors and whispers travelled faster than cars. By the time the first trucks arrived from the north, the newcomers would be seen as Genghis and his cavalry, ready to rape and plunder. If they were capable of torching their own loved ones, the invaders were definitely capable of repeating the crimes against their new neighbors. Who would want to live surrounded by people they didn't trust, people they know were capable of barbarity?

Having read enough, he opened his email and started typing.

Mom and Dad,

I'm sure by now you've heard what happened. I wanted to let you know I'm not among the people traveling south to Washington. I wasn't at the stadium, but Katherine was. And she took Galen there. I couldn't stand to see her again so I left. Right now I'm north of New York City, but I'm not settling down here.

I know you'll probably worry about me when you read this, but I'd rather be by myself than with those people. I wish you both the best. No one could have asked for better, more loving parents. I hope the Florida sun is treating you well. I love you both. I'll write again.

Jeffrey

There were a lot of other things he thought about saying. They could be said in future letters, however. When he finished typing he powered off the computer. There had been no email from Katherine asking where he was or if he would be returning. It was doubtful there ever would be.

He passed a string of little towns where trees had fallen into homes. Even the houses that missed being hit had collapsed roofs because of the winters and the storms. Everywhere he went, the roads were battered. Only eighty miles north of home, abandoned by the masses for only three years, the roads looked like a series of massive earthquakes must have ripped the land apart. Philadelphia would look the same way in two or three years. Another few years after that and Washington would be the same. Everything would be, eventually.

Ahead of him, a mile up the road, he saw something on the side of the highway that didn't resemble the abandoned cars and flat tires he was used to seeing. It wasn't until he was within twenty feet of it that he realized it was a body. Not once had he seen a dead animal on the road in the short span of his trip—there simply weren't enough vehicles traveling the roads anymore, and the ones that did were moving too slowly to hit anything. Now, instead of a deer or raccoon, lay the body of an actual person.

"Lord, help me," Jeffrey muttered to himself.

The tank stopped five feet from the body. *Whoever it was would be dead*, he thought, *there's no point to rushing out to provide medical assistance*.

Part of him didn't want to stop at all, but he did. The thing that kept Jeffrey there, in the middle of the highway, was the placement of the body. It wasn't splayed out like a run-down animal; the body's arms were by its side as though someone had simply dragged it out of a car and left it there. One of the people from the monster truck caravan must have ditched it.

He kept staring at it, wondering if the body was on the side of the road because whoever it was had already died, and transporting them any further would have been wasted space. Or was it a Block who had been abandoned when it became too much of a burden? The body—a young man—looked to be the same age as Galen.

This last thought compelled him to climb out and inspect it. Tiny lines of ants were making their way up and down the man's skin. There was nothing to differentiate the body to know for sure if it had been a regular person or a Block. It was the Block's life that separated it from normal people, not its death.

As Jeffrey looked at the body, the only thing he could think about was Galen. Galen lying there on the ground. Galen being abandoned. Galen needing love. Galen on fire. Galen as a singed skeleton.

If only he hadn't convinced Katherine to have a baby in the first place. The years afterwards would have been quiet and lonely without his son there, but the twenty years of not being a father would have been worth it if he didn't have to know his boy was burned to death.

Flies came and went from the man's body. Given time, maggots would work away at anything the birds and foxes didn't nibble on first. The skin would begin to smell awful.

Thinking back to the cars passing by him in that

caravan, he thought about all of the drivers who hadn't looked his way, didn't smile or wave, only continued south in the direction they felt they needed to go. One of them had just recently pulled their son, this boy, out of their vehicle just long enough to ditch the body at the roadside before speeding ahead to rejoin the rest of the caravan.

Just then, with Jeffrey only two feet away, the man blinked.

"Fuck," Jeffrey screamed, falling backwards.

And yet there was no flicker of recognition from the body on the ground, no relief at being saved, not even uncomprehending blinking of trying to figure out if he was alive or if he was already in the afterlife. The eyes closed again. That was the man's only movement. And Jeffrey knew that this was the only movement the body ever had and ever would make.

Physically, it would have been easy to wave the monster trucks ahead and let the rest of the cars go by. But how could you actually do that to another person, just leave them there? Maybe the driver had acted as though they were changing another flat tire until the caravan disappeared over a hill. Then they would take the Block under his armpits and drag him onto the road. The car would smell better as soon as the unchanged diapers were no longer there. But to simply abandon your flesh and blood on the side of the highway, to let this man starve to death, if the elements didn't get him first, how could you drive away from that, rejoining the caravan as though nothing had happened?

If only I hadn't let my boy out of my sight, Jeffrey thought.

Unsure of what to do, he simply stood over the body. There was no way he could keep driving as if he had never found this young man. If nothing else, he had to at least give the man a blanket and some water. That wasn't enough either, though. The Block would never know if it was suffering from dehydration, would never shiver from the cold, but that didn't mean it was acceptable to leave it to the frigid nights. He went back to the tank and when he approached the body again he had blankets and a bottle of water. He unrolled the blanket, pulling it up around the Block's shoulders. Then he unscrewed the water bottle and poured a sip's worth into the man's mouth. The water dribbled out the sides of his lips. Jeffrey hadn't manually fed a Block since Galen was a little boy. The thought made him groan.

If only Katherine would have trusted me that everything would be OK.

He sat with the young man on the side of the road. It was just him and the Block for as far as he could see. Nothing else.

There were a lot of things he could do. He could race back and catch up to the group. But for what, to search for one family within the caravan? To have them feel ashamed for a day or a week until they abandoned the Block again a few days later? You don't abandon somebody once and then take it all back.

He could go back to Newark and try to find the man who had been left behind by the caravan. But why would that man want the burden of this Block? And if the man was foolhardy enough to wait in the middle of the highway until he was too hungry and thirsty to save himself, this Block was just as well here on the side of the road as he would be sitting next to the other man's dead daughter.

He could take the young man with him. But surely, it was a matter of time until the Block died. What was the difference between the Block dying here or dying further north? No living person would turn to Jeffrey and say, "Oh sure, just strap me to the back of your tank and check on me every hundred miles. Oh, and if a bird shits on me, would you be a good chap and clean it off? Thanks!"

So he sat with the young man, the tank remaining in the middle lane of the highway. How comical it would be if there were still police officers around and one came across a random tank in the middle of the road during his daily patrol. Now, the police cars were just as likely to be abandoned as any other mid-size car.

He put his ear to the Block's mouth to listen for how often the man was taking breaths. The breathing was so faint Jeffrey couldn't hear anything at all. He kept his fingers on the Block's wrist to feel for a pulse. It was soft, barely enough to register, but it was there.

"Don't worry," Jeffrey said as he unwrapped his own blanket, lying down only four feet away from where the Block was underneath the other blanket.

If only this were my boy and not a random body. I would trade anything if this were Galen.

Closing his eyes from the light gave him a chance to collect his thoughts. Since leaving Fort Dix with the tank, all he had was time to himself. Yet, he had never taken the opportunity to stop and really think. Instead, he let the tank drown out the yells and torments in his mind. The only problem was, once there was quiet, he didn't like the thoughts that started racing around. He begged God to bring his boy back, to take him instead, if it meant Galen could be alive again. He cursed Katherine and her fear. He cursed the world. When the thoughts became too much, he rubbed his eyes until they hurt, then opened them once more to the sunlight.

With the body there next to him, he had nothing to

do but sit and wait. He thought about telling the Block a story, but the true things about his life—Galen, his wife, the fire—all hurt too much. The only other stories he could think of all involved the horrors of being a Block. One of the men at work had kept insisting there was a man in Chicago who had refused to leave after the city was abandoned. The old man rounded up all the Blocks he could find and rode the subway with them all day, back and forth from one end of the line, to the other, the entire train full of silent passengers. The train would go south until it reached Chicago's south side. Hundreds of Blocks filling the seats. And then the man would pull a different lever and the train would make its way back through the city until it got to the north end. Day after day, the old man travelled this way, transporting hundreds of Blocks through the city. One by one, the Blocks would eventually die. But still, the old man drove the train back and forth until the entire subway line was a ghost train filled with rotting corpses. It was the type of story you were supposed to tell children at campfires, not the type you told to a Block unless you were an asshole.

If he was going to sit on the side of the road, he needed to find some books to read. It was that or sit and watch the clouds pass by. The Block's eyes were open again, pointed toward the sky. If the young man had once possessed good vision, the sun would have blinded him by now. Jeffrey leaned over and pushed the Block's face so his head was looking to his side, away from the sun.

He sat up and checked the Block's pulse again, still barely there, before pouring more water into his mouth. The water would only prolong the man's suffering—if he could suffer—but not giving him water would be like sitting around letting another person die for no reason.

His belly was starting to protest, but it wasn't fair to get food while the Block starved to death in front of him.

He closed his eyes in hopes that when he opened them again the Block would have passed away.

It was the middle of the night when he woke the next time. Again, he reached over to feel for the Block's pulse.

"Jesus Christ. What are you hanging on for? What's worth fighting for?"

When he woke up the next morning, ants had covered the Block's eyes and mouth. He brushed them off and put a damp cloth over the young man's face to keep them away. Each time he touched the man's wrist he expected the tiny beating to have stopped. Each time, though, the faintest of patters tapped against his fingertip. He climbed into the tank, where he felt less guilty about eating while another man starved. As soon as he chewed the last bit of sandwich, he climbed back out and rejoined the Block.

"It should be a beautiful day."

They stayed like that, in silence, for an hour before Jeffrey spoke again.

"I don't know how you're doing it. I'd have died after the first night. What point are you trying to prove?"

He snuck back to the tank later in the day for another sandwich. Any time he had a drink of water, he also poured a sip into the Block's mouth. The drops of water splashed in and around cracked, blistered lips.

He spent part of the day reading the few documents left inside the tank. For an hour he actually read the tank's standard operating procedures. For another hour he walked around the highway, always keeping the tank and the body in sight. When he awoke from his next nap, he again checked the young man's pulse. It was still there.

"What are you trying to prove? What's keeping you here? Just go. Put yourself out of your misery. You don't owe these people anything."

Yet, there was no sense of pain or anguish on the other man's face. It was Jeffrey who was shouting and irritated, not the dying, starving Block.

Before going to sleep, he snuck inside the tank and had the last of the sandwiches. He woke up in the middle of the night expecting the body beside him to finally be cold, but the heart was still beating, and he groaned and wished he could be spending these nights under the stars with Galen.

The next day, he finally reached over, touched the man's wrist, and felt nothing. No beat. No life. The young man's family would never have any idea how long their Block brother or son had fought to stay alive. Would they have acted differently if they knew how long it would take for this man to fade away? Probably not.

A body was on the ground, as peaceful in death as it had been in life. Never once could it complain about its circumstances. The young man had never been able to think: *If only I had different parents. If only I had been normal. If only they had understood that I wouldn't make them sick; I was just another person trying to get by each day.*

He thought to bury the young man, but didn't have a shovel. A warrior's pyre was possible, but the thought of starting any fire, let alone one in which to burn a Block, made him shake uncontrollably. In the end, he arranged the body so it was flat on its back, arms by its side. He covered it first with one of the blankets, then with a collection of sticks and leaves. The Block deserved more than simply being left to rot under the sun, but he didn't know what else he could do for it.

An animal would come along in the next day or two, pull the blanket away, and start eating the body. The peaceful pose would be ruined as the wolf or bear dragged and tore the carcass apart.

The tank's engine roared to life. As much as Jeffrey tried to convince himself the water and blanket had been all he could offer, he thought about everything else he might have done if it were Galen on the side of the road. He would have talked to the boy all night long. He would have forced food down his son's throat. He would have found a way to give his son a proper burial.

As the tank continued north, he tried not to think of Galen's burnt flesh or of how long remnants of his son's charred body would remain in the open air.

Chapter 7

People never stopped whispering that if you spent too much time around Blocks, you could become a Block yourself. It never happened, but the old wives' tale persisted and kept people scared. A dot-com billionaire was so fearful of the possibility that he decided to escape to the one place his money could take him and only him: outer space. As soon as the Great De-evolution started, he left his offices in Silicon Valley and paid just over one billion dollars to have a Russian aeronautical company build him a space shuttle. The shuttle, he told his wife and kids, was only big enough for one person. His plan was to return as soon as a cure for the Blocks was discovered or a vaccine was created to prevent regular people from turning into part of the quiet masses.

Having the spaceship built was the easy part. It was more of a pod, really, than a ship. After the rocket carried it up into space, the roughly ten foot by ten foot room would give him just enough headway to live out his days. A modified version of the food processors, less than half the size of the regular version, was installed in the pod. He was given an extra small power generator as well. After the toilet and bed were installed, there wasn't much room left.

But while armies of scientists all around the world labored to find a way to stop the Great De-evolution, none of them bothered to work on a vaccine because they all knew the Block condition was something you couldn't catch. The "Block disease" was an urban legend, like the man riding the Chicago subway, meant to scare you once the lights were off, nothing more.

So the billionaire stayed in space. His family remained in constant contact with him. Each time he asked if a cure had been found, they shook their heads. The billionaire orbited earth again and again, receiving the same answer each time he spoke to his wife and kids. But then a transmission wasn't made from the pod one night. The next day's transmission was also skipped. The family told the media how concerned they were. The billionaire was never heard from again.

The heart monitor he wore, originally thought to have malfunctioned, told everyone he had suffered a major heart attack while orbiting somewhere over Kenya. And for the rest of time, as the world's population got older and older, as the billionaire's wife died, then, eventually, his children, and even later, the very last people in the final settlements, the billionaire's dead body kept circling Earth over and over again. As dead as everyone below it.

On clear nights, you could still take your telescope outside and, at just the right time, catch a glimpse of the billionaire's tiny shuttle passing in front of the moon. On cloudy nights, death is still orbiting the planet, you just can't see it.

These were the types of stories Jeffrey and Katherine never spoke about. The nights he did see the pod drift by in front of the moon, he didn't point it out to her. It became another topic, along with whether or not having Galen had been the right decision, that they couldn't talk about to each other.

Although he never voiced his thoughts, he could never completely stop wondering how things would have been different if they had tried having a baby earlier in their marriage. Every time he had tried to convince her, she had balked. Every time he had tried to bargain with her, she had walked away from the table. It was almost guaranteed that

Galen would have been born normal if Katherine had gotten pregnant when she was twenty. Waiting until she was thirty, when the epidemic of Blocks had wiped out any good chance of having a regular baby, just didn't make sense. Why couldn't she ever admit that all of her complaints could have been squashed if she'd just trusted him earlier? He still remembered having to beg, literally, on both knees, saying stupid things like, "I'll never ask you for another thing if we do this," or "If you agree to this, I'll do a hundred percent of the diaper changing."

If only he could have convinced her to believe in him earlier. He still sat up some nights wondering what he could have said, what agreement he could have made or what confidence he could have instilled in her that would have gotten her to agree just a little bit sooner. Why had she fought him over it, why had she delayed, just to eventually give in?

He didn't like to think about the other side: what if they hadn't had a child at all? So focused was he on the idea that they should have become parents earlier that he didn't allow the other possibility to seem feasible. Each time he was on one side of the house, wondering why it had taken so long to convince her, she had been, at the very same moment, on the other end of the house asking herself why she couldn't have held out just a year or two longer.

Each time he thought Katherine might bring the topic up, he took Galen outside on the porch for the evening. And no matter how many times he sat outside and listened to the birds with his son, no matter how many times he noticed the dead billionaire's pod as it passed in front of the moon, he never realized there was more than one way to escape your fears. You didn't have to fly to outer space; you could simply walk to another room.

**

Further up the road, he came to a bridge, only two or three hundred feet in length, that was entirely gone. Only a single beam remained to offer a reminder of what had been there. Truly, a bridge to nowhere. Down at the bank of the river he saw rusted support beams that had snagged against the embankment and refused to wash out to the ocean after the bridge collapsed.

His map said there was another bridge, slightly west of this one. That second one, when he came upon it, was intact and easy to cross. On the other side, he came to a park with trees lining a river. The birds' chirping could be heard even before he powered the tank's engine off. As much as he tried, he couldn't stop thinking about sitting on the porch with his boy.

If only the people had been less scared. If only he had listened to Katherine and taken his family south earlier. None of this would have happened.

He watched a squirrel pack its mouth full of nuts before scampering to the top of a tree. Winter would be coming soon. Without his own plan for where he would be when it did arrive, he found himself wondering instead where Katherine might be when it got cold. A colony of ants took turns carrying crumbs from his sandwich. He had always thought of these little creatures as being clueless, completely oblivious to everything except the immediate world around them. The truth was they all had a better plan than he did. The birds migrated south for the winter. The squirrels hibernated. Who knew what the ants did? But they surely had some scheme because they were here now and would be again the next summer. And, more importantly, they would be here long after man was gone.

He rode northeast the rest of the day, ending up in the city of New Haven. He spent the night in an abandoned hotel room, then the next day roaming the streets.

The windows of an old supermarket were boarded up. Most likely, a storm had come through all the way back when people still lived here, but the owner had known it was a matter of time until they traveled south and that replacing the windows would be a waste. The front door was still unlocked, and the shelves still had some old cans of food. He missed walking by the bakery near his house and smelling warm chocolate chip cookies, cinnamon bagels, and fresh loaves of bread.

After breakfast, he toured the museums and historic buildings. Old paintings still littered the museum walls; no one had bothered to protect them or take them on the trip south when the city was vacated. At the water's edge, there was a sign for a famous old boat that was no longer there. Either it had sunk to the bottom of the bay or someone had been foolhardy enough to attempt the journey south on a creaky, historic relic rather than a modern vessel.

After being in the tank for so long it was nice to spend the day doing nothing but walking. As he made his way through the city, he saw a car upside down in the road, a suitcase hanging from a lamppost, and a cemetery entrance with a bright red X painted on it. There was never an explanation for these things, and he chalked it all up to the madness of slowly becoming extinct.

An electronics store had working computers and an internet connection. They probably had working phones too, but he didn't want to talk to his parents or anyone he knew. He wasn't ready for that. What he could handle were their written words.

<u>Jeffrey,</u>

Do you remember the cardinal you found in the backyard when you were a little boy? You were six years old. I remember your age because you were seven when you lost your front teeth and that hadn't happened yet. Parents don't forget those things. Anyway, you came in crying because its wing was broken and it couldn't fly away. You wanted to run over and pick it up because you were a child and thought that if you could just carry it back inside the house, your father and I could make everything better. But when you got close to it and reached to pick it up, it screamed and tried to fly away even though it couldn't get off the ground. I still remember how hard you cried when this little thing, in its terror, was hurting itself even worse because it couldn't understand that you just wanted to help it. That screaming bird gave you nightmares for a month.

To make you feel better, we told you that your father took it to the vet, where its wing was healed and it flew away a couple of weeks later. Our lie did the trick: you cheered up and you believed the bird was somewhere better. I still cringe when I remember how angry you got, as a teenager, when you demanded to know the truth. Years went by without you thinking about that bird again, but something at school one day must have triggered those memories because you came home with the realization that our story was a little too nice. I was so sad to see my little boy demand the truth even though it would upset you. Probably, you wanted to hear it just because you knew it would upset you. Teenagers are a pain in the ass that way.

Anyway, your father finally admitted he broke the bird's neck and buried it in the backyard. He barely got the confession out before you started yelling at us. If you had yelled at us like that for any other reason, you would have been grounded until your next birthday, but there was something at the core of what was upsetting you that we couldn't punish. After seven years, you still wanted justice for the poor little bird that had somehow broken its wing and needed help but was too scared to be saved.

You didn't care at the time that your father hated himself for what he had to do. He couldn't even punish Critter when the damn dog wouldn't stop barking. You should have seen his shoulders collapse when he realized he had to put the poor bird out of its misery. The same nights you were having nightmares about the cardinal, your father was lying awake in bed, unable to sleep because even though he wanted to help it, just like you had wanted to, he couldn't.

When I think about that story now, I don't think about our lie or about how angry you were when you found out the truth, or even about the effect it had on your father. I think about the one thing that was more important than anything else: my little boy saw an animal that was hurting and all he wanted to do was help it. Nothing else mattered.

You will find, as you get older, that the key to being happy is being able to turn those bad memories into treasured ones. I used to cringe at the thought of you being so angry with us. Now, you couldn't give me all the gold in the world to take that memory away, because it reminds me of the type of person you were and still are.

And now you have to help yourself, however it is you think that's possible. Nothing else matters.

We love you. Be safe. We don't say that as parents simply wanting the best for our son, we say it as the mother and father that saw you cry because you wanted to pick up a defenseless animal and save it.

He didn't reply then because he didn't know what to say. If she had been there in the computer store, he would put his arms around her and hugged her until they were both done crying. Instead, he could do nothing but power down the computer and turn the store lights off.

Eventually, he found the local library and spent the day looking through shelf after shelf of dusty books. By the time he walked through the first three rows he already had a stack he wanted to take with him. Instead of loading the entire stack in the tank, then stocking up on even more, he put most of the books down, taking only the two he most wanted to read, and left the others on the shelf closest to the entrance for the next time he stopped by.

An old radio was sitting by the librarian's desk. He flipped it on to hear static. Slowly turning the dial, he found four stations with music still playing on a loop. No real, live human voices ever came on the air. Everything else, besides the cycle of music beginning again every ninety minutes, was static.

A house on the beach gave him a clear view of the waves and the ocean. The grocery stores gave him natural food to mix in with what the food processor produced. He had access to all the books he could ask for. And he had a reprieve from the tank. After a long day inside the machine, he couldn't stand up straight for ten minutes. After weeks of traveling inside it, he was sure he looked like the Hunchback of Notre Dame.

The leaves were turning color and beginning to fall. He would stay at the beach through winter. Each night he looked out at the ocean, watching the waves crash until only the light from the moon kept them visible. If the clouds were covering the moon, only the sound of crashing water let him know the ocean was still there.

Instead of sitting on the porch with Galen every night, he imagined taking his son to the beach.

If only my boy could be here to see this with me.

Over and over he thought that.

He even included Katherine in his hopes. Maybe, if they had lived on the beach, where people didn't rush around from appointment to appointment, cursing the rush hour traffic and the red lights, she would have understood that going south wasn't the most important thing in the world. With the ocean in front of her instead of steel buildings, maybe she would have been more reassured that the world wasn't some place you needed to fear.

She had lost something over the years. That was the difference between the person he had fallen in love with and the person who was singularly focused on getting to Washington. What was that thing, invisible and untouchable, that was gone? She had still believed good things happened to good people and bad things happened to bad people. What else was there—her loyalty, her priorities? Something had faded away over the years, something that left her seeming like the person he had loved and married, but made her capable of taking their son to a stadium full of strangers.

When he found himself thinking about her and Galen, he closed the book he was reading and went for another walk. The waves crashed no matter what time of year it was, no matter what time of day it was. That was what he liked about them—their reliability, calming and reassuring.

The entire winter was spent that way. Sometimes the snow kept him inside for a week straight. During those stretches, he found himself constantly trying to think what he could have done to change the past, to think of something he might do differently so his boy would still be alive. Other times, he bundled up and went for a walk during the heaviest storms because he liked feeling the crunch of snow and sand mixing together under his boots.

And he read every book the library had that had won the Hugo Award. When he was done with them, he started reading every book in their collection that had won the Booker Award. By the time he finished each one, he felt he had learned something else about the world. Week after week went by that way.

Finally, the snow stopped falling and, eventually, disappeared from the ground so that only the sand remained.

A stack of unread books was already sitting inside the machine, an equally big stack of peanut butter and jelly sandwiches next to them. The tank started up like it always did. He started moving north again.

Chapter 8

"They're saying we have too many Blocks to be able to transport all of them."

"Who's saying that?"

But the skeleton never answered the other man's questions.

"They're saying Providence didn't have this high of a ratio of Blocks to regular people when they moved, and they still had trouble."

"Who said that?"

"Remember, we have all of New York's Blocks now too. They're saying if we try to leave with this many, it will be at the expense of the people who can actually talk—at the expense of the people who have been kind enough to care for the Blocks!"

That was all it took for half of the audience before they stopped listening; they were already packing their bags. It was critical that they distanced themselves from the obvious disaster that was going to unfold as the caravan left for Washington.

The 120 miles between Philadelphia and Washington wasn't far by traditional standards. But no one could measure the effect of adding five hundred buses full of people who couldn't help change a flat tire. And then you had to add another hundred buses on top of that just to carry the supplies needed to take care of those people. Each additional consideration was another potential delay. The possible hold-ups grew exponentially with each person sitting in each bus.

Jeffrey was just thankful the skeleton hadn't used the grocery store analogy again. It had terrified Katherine enough the first time.

With his gaunt cheeks and hollow eyes, he would look right into the camera and tell people that transporting Blocks to another city was really no different than taking them shopping for food. He would pause for a moment before explaining why that should be so disturbing. It might take a single person half an hour to go grocery shopping, he would say. It might take a pair of people forty minutes because they want to stop and talk about their options. A group of ten people would take an hour in the same store. And with that many people, a jar or a drink would be dropped, glass shattered, and an announcement made on the intercom that a cleanup was needed in aisle seven. A group of twenty people might as well plan to spend the entire night in the grocery store. Now turn those twenty people into a hundred thousand and tell them they have to change cities instead of simply shop for ingredients for dinner.

Jeffrey was used to people saying the Blocks weren't really people, just shells of people. Not a single day passed that he didn't hear a new joke about the Blocks. Everyone who had ever made a Polack joke changed focus and began making fun of the people responsible for the end of mankind.

If a tree falls in the woods and no one is around to hear it... can it at least fall on a Block?

How many Blocks does it take to change a light bulb? I don't know, I'm still waiting for one of them to tell me.

What do you get when you combine a Block with a blonde? The best date of your life.

When these things were said on TV, Jeffrey turned the power off. If a neighbor or co-worker said it, he turned his back and didn't talk to them the rest of the week.

On his way to Fort Dix, he passed an old billboard that used to say 'Make Dairy an important part of your diet.' Most of that old message was gone, however. The new writing said, "Blocks are NOT an important part of our lives." He thought about simply ramming one of the wooden supports elevating the billboard, causing it to collapse on the side of the road. His car would be totaled, but he could leave it there and start driving one of the abandoned cars all around him.

The billboards were just part of the problem; there were more and more fliers stapled to telephone poles and taped to stop signs. None of them were complimentary to the Blocks. The fliers were created by different groups, each with a different level of hatred, but they all suggested—or flat out proclaimed—that Blocks weren't really people at all, and didn't need the normal consideration given to everyone else. We aren't taking the city's supply of mannequins with us, the pamphlets would say, so why are we determined to take the Blocks? At least a mannequin could be disassembled and thrown in a box. Jeffrey tore these down as he walked past them. Two city blocks later, he would have a stack of them in his hands.

Knock, knock. Who's there? Block. Block who? Take care of me for the rest of your life and find out.

When he showed up to work after missing a day, instead of being asked if he was feeling better or asking if he had some unplanned emergency, he was greeted by everyone saying, "I figured you'd left." He didn't blame them, it was the first thought he had each time someone else didn't show up to work too.

He turned to see one of the other remaining

lieutenants coming back for a refill of coffee. The man had long ago forsaken his uniform. For the past two years, he showed up to work in khakis and ugly Hawaiian shirts. He was only outdone by the lieutenant colonel who decided the Great De-evolution meant it was finally time to get the earrings and tattoos he had always wanted.

"I figured we'd never see you again," the man said.

Of course, Jeffrey could have avoided all the explanations if he had listened to Katherine and simply called off instead of just not showing up. Although this, too, had been done by some of the men skipping town, as though calling out sick and then heading south would give them a head start before the military police came looking for them—no one had been arrested for leaving their post since the beginning of the Great De-evolution.

Sir, I'm not paying for a mime who just sits there. That's not a mime, it's my Block brother—the mime is over there.

Priorities reset themselves as the world's population shrank. Workplace snafus, no matter how important they may have seemed before, were taken as minor infractions. Jeffrey would learn that even workplace violence was sometimes excused.

He was still in his early thirties at the time, old enough to understand adult responsibilities, but still young enough to get heated like an out-of-control teenager. The write-up had occurred after he showed up to work following Galen's birth. Most of the men had sympathized with Jeffrey's situation as the parent of a newborn Block. But there were a select few who didn't approve of anyone trying to have kids once the Blocks appeared.

One such man was Sonny. If you were in the middle of telling a story about getting a speeding ticket, Sonny was the guy who said you shouldn't have been driving so fast. Everything could have been prevented if you just managed to be a little less stupid, a little more like Sonny.

"Where you been?" Sonny had said upon seeing Jeffrey in the office kitchen.

"Had a kid."

That was how conversations went around Sonny because no one wanted to talk to the man. Everything he said made you want to punch the closest thing you could find, and Sonny's biggest problem was that he was often the closest thing.

"What would make you want to have a kid these days? Chances are it's gonna be a Block."

Jeffrey turned and started back toward his office.

But Sonny followed close behind. "So is it safe to assume your kid is a Block?"

"Yes, my son is a Block," Jeffrey said.

"Just great. Another kid we'll all have to take care of when you get too old to do it yourself." Not even that was enough to hit another man, but Sonny wouldn't stop: "I gotta hand it to you, you got a big set of balls to have a kid when it's almost guaranteed he'd be retar—"

Sonny's next word was cut off by Jeffrey tackling him. On top of the cheap, industrial military carpet that doubled as sandpaper, Jeffrey held Sonny's face against the ground with one hand while he punched him with his other hand. One side of Sonny's face was rubbed raw from carpet burns, the other side was quickly covered in bruises and blood.

Roses are red, violets are blue, your Block is boring, and so are you.

Jeffrey would have thought one of the other men would pull him off of Sonny. Instead, he continued throwing punch after punch while straddling the helpless, screaming bully. Other men had gathered around, but they just stood and watched. Maybe they needed a distraction from their own daily sorrows. Maybe they just wanted to see Sonny finally get his comeuppance. It was only when Jeffrey's boss at the time, a colonel named Baker, came around the corner and saw what was going on that Jeffrey was ordered to stop.

No one offered to help Sonny back up to his feet. Someone in the crowd whooped with excitement as though they were back in high school and the principal had interrupted some good entertainment between classes.

When he got home, Katherine saw his bloody knuckles and asked what had happened. He hadn't even had a chance to say hello or ask what was for dinner. Instead of yelling at him, she put her arms around him and told him everything would be all right. His head went immediately to her shoulder. Before he could get a single word out he was sobbing. She held him against her, her hands rubbing him so he almost melted.

"Shh, it's OK," she kept saying over and over, which only made him cry harder. "Everything is going to be OK."

Other than that episode, he was the one holding her while she cried. He perfected the approach after Galen was born and she had a hard time adjusting to having a son who couldn't speak or move but was otherwise healthy. She had cried a lot in those first months. A little since, but a lot in the early days.

He had gone straight to Baker's office the next day without having to be told to report there for whatever punishment was in store. With the world seeming to fade away before everyone's eyes, he had no idea what kind of reprimand to expect. How were the base's leaders supposed to deal with issues in the midst of more officers sneaking away each day to take their families south?

"We're all in this together," Baker had started. "We all know we aren't going to be here much longer."

That was the extent of Baker's speech. He didn't explain if he meant Fort Dix was eventually going to be shut down, the way the Navy's base in Connecticut already had, the way all military installations would eventually turn into ghost towns, or if he meant that not a single human would be on the earth much longer. There was no long lecture about how an officer should conduct himself. He didn't bother threatening a dishonorable discharge or a missed promotion.

As Jeffrey was leaving the office, Baker added, "That asshole certainly had it coming."

"Thank you, sir."

Jeffrey was expecting one of the men to tell him Sonny had a couple of minor injuries; he wasn't expecting to be told of a broken nose, jaw, and eye socket. He also wasn't expecting to hear that while Jeffrey had not gotten in any trouble, the remaining brass had told Sonny not to bother reporting to work again, that his kind wasn't needed anymore.

He liked to think Sonny would have actually liked being around Galen if they had gotten the chance to meet. What more could a self-centered guy want than someone who would let him talk as much as he wanted? Galen was the perfect audience for any bad jokes or complaints about your awful day or your unhappy life.

A priest, a rabbi, and a Block walk into a bar... oh wait, no, the Block is still sitting wherever the priest and rabbi left him.

**

He went north along the eastern side of a peninsula. The waves seemed to be calling to him. Parts of the road gave him such a clear view of the ocean that he considered pulling over and walking into the water and giving up his journey.

The map showed a bridge further up the road that would take him east. He prayed the mile-long structure hadn't collapsed yet. But then it came in sight and part of him wished it had deteriorated so he didn't have to cross it. The structure was intact, but after getting out and inspecting it closer, he saw parts where the pavement had crumbled completely away and water could be seen hundreds of feet below.

Maybe this bridge would last another year, or maybe it was already ruined and he just wouldn't realize it until the tank was plummeting toward the ocean below. He had no idea if it would even support a car anymore, let alone something as heavy as an entire line of cars. *So be it*, he thought, trying to convince himself that falling into the ocean was as good an end as any other. It was, certainly, better than his son had been given.

His mind presented him with every scenario in which he didn't make it across the bridge. He could travel ten feet and then have the bridge collapse. The structure might support him until he was almost all the way across before dropping him into the ocean. Maybe the structure would last long enough as it fell apart for him to jump out and run for safety. Or maybe it would collapse as soon as he raised the hatch and looked out. He would be falling before he knew what was happening. The more he thought of it, the more it terrified him.

Even if he did make it all the way across, he would only be on land for two miles before coming to Newport Bridge, a two-mile structure that dwarfed this one. If he made it over this first bridge, only to find the second one washed away, he would have to turn around and hope he could make it all the way across the first mile-long path, or risk being stuck in between the two waterways on a tiny island for the rest of his life.

As a young man, he had imagined himself becoming a grandfather, getting grey hair and growing old while his grandchildren darted past him. He did not imagine himself dying on some little, deserted island he had never heard of before. And he certainly didn't think he would meet his end after crashing into the water (in a tank!) from three hundred feet above. The tank inched forward until half of its weight rested at the very beginning of the structure, then, after a minute, the entire thing.

"Well, no time like the present," he said and the tank lurched forward.

He kept expecting to hear the concrete crumble, the steel cables to snap, before feeling himself become weightless, free-falling toward the ocean below. Just the thought made his lunch want to come up his throat. As he fell, he would want to take a breath but be unable to do so. His head became light at the idea.

Every few seconds he thought he heard a pop or a bang and expected to feel himself falling. Each time, he grabbed hold of the steering levers until his knuckles were white.

It took the tank an eternity to reach the bridge's crest. Jeffrey's arms were shaking. His fingers ached. He felt sick to his stomach. And then, finally, the tank started down the other side. He prayed for the land to get closer, faster.

And then the shore approached. He'd never been so happy to see a rocky beach. The tank was on land again.

Part of him wanted an excuse to linger on the island between the two bridges so he wouldn't have to face the next expanse so soon. At that moment, crossing another bridge seemed as good an idea as a second round of Russian Roulette.

Already, the next structure was approaching. Unlike the first one, being fairly flat, this one took him in the air right away. He had no idea how high the bridge was at its peak, but just seeing it made his fingers start trembling again. How long would it take from the time the bridge gave way and the tank started falling to the time it hit water? That was the worst part. He wasn't afraid of drowning inside the tank as it sank to the bottom of the ocean; he was afraid of the air being sucked out of his chest as he fell through the sky, helpless.

His chest began to burn.

He drove past an abandoned minivan, two of its four tires missing. Further up the bridge, he passed the torn remains of shredded rubber. That must have been the point where a family had given up and decided to attempt the rest of the journey by foot.

The idea lingered in the back of his head that he could rev the tank's engine to full speed and outrace the collapsing structure if it was falling from underneath him. It had been done a thousand times in action movies. The thought was fantasy, however. If he had the misfortune of feeling the structure give way underneath him as it started to fall into the ocean, he would be going with it. The machine could go faster than he had imagined, but it could never outrace time or decay or gravity.

The land seemed to disappear completely as the tank pointed toward the sky. He imagined getting halfway across the bridge, only to have a small section at the very middle be missing, and then to have a section behind him dislodge after the tank rode over it. That part of the bridge would fall into the water too. He would be on a tiny sliver of pavement, suspended hundreds of feet in the air, a mile from land on either side. The thought made him wish he were wearing one of Galen's diapers.

The tank passed a pair of old bicycles strewn across the bridge like a pitiful roadblock. At one time, they had probably been Christmas presents for happy children. Where are those happy children now, he wondered? Will they ever remember how excited they were to receive those bicycles on that cold winter morning? The tank ran over both bikes, leaving behind a jumbled heap of aluminum.

Further along the bridge he saw an old American flag, faded under the sun, tied to the bridge's railing. Anyone riding a boat underneath the bridge would have looked up and remembered the pride and history of the land they were in. Was a British flag hanging over the Thames? Was a French flag hanging over the Seine? Maybe they were. He liked to think they were.

Just when he thought the bridge might keep going into the sky forever, it flattened out, then began a gentle slope back toward the earth. Looking down at the water, far enough below that individual waves could no longer be seen, he thought back to the daredevils who used to attach bungee cords to themselves and fall hundreds of feet for sheer fun. That was a long time ago, before people began migrating south. Why did he always have to think about those types of things?

Finally, the tank was on solid ground again. He let out a long, relieved sigh.

From his map he knew he could veer right and pass a pond so large it should be a lake. A bird sanctuary was also there. But to see those things he would have to cross a third bridge, and his interest in crossing bridges was gone.

His route took him by one golf course, then another, and then yet another. He had already lost track of how many golf courses he had passed on his journey. Each one was overgrown, more a nicely shaped field of weeds than eighteen holes of sport.

Where were all of the men who used to spend their precious days away from work riding a cart from hole to hole? If they had known what was coming, how would they have spent their time instead? For no other reason than he could, he turned off the road and gunned the tank's engine to full speed. It's tread tore up the 7th fairway, the 8th hole's green, and then a sand bunker. And then, like nothing had happened, he veered the tank back on the highway and continued north.

He came to a bridge that was so small it didn't appear on his map. This one was only twenty or thirty feet long. Of course, this was the one that was destroyed.

"Are you kidding me?" he said.

A third of the bridge was gone. He pulled the tank to the edge of the crevice before getting out and inspecting the scene. Looking down, he saw the crumbled remains of what used to connect his side of the bridge with the other side. The drop from the bridge to the ground looked to be around fifteen feet.

For a while, he did nothing but rub his chin in slow circles while his mind worked. Some abandoned cars were nearby. A collection of houses was in the distance. The sun was directly overhead.

"All right then," he said, "Let's get the show on the road."

He moved the tank away from the bridge. Next, he walked to the first abandoned car, a four-door sedan that looked to be in perfect shape, except two tires were completely gone. The keys were still in the ignition. After being inside the tank exclusively, it felt odd to be sitting in a cushioned chair with his legs out in front of him, so low to the ground. When he shifted the transmission into drive, the car scraped across the ground. He took it toward the gap in the bridge. Even at such a slow speed, the metal wheels whined against the concrete and little sparks kicked off the ground. With the car at the edge of the gap, he got out and pushed as hard as he could until the front two tires fell over the edge. The car's weight released from his pressure and dropped into the void. It landed face-first on the ground, then rolled over on its top so two tires and two metal wheels stuck in the air like a surrendering dog.

With the car settled in the abyss, he went to the next abandoned vehicle, an old Jeep without any doors, and did the same thing with it. The third abandoned car wouldn't start. And there was no way he could push it the entire distance to the void. There were two more abandoned cars a hundred yards down the road from where he had come. He walked there, drove one of them to the edge of the pit, pushed it in, then walked back for the second car and did the same thing again.

An odd thing happened as he pushed each car into position: he became angrier and angrier. With the sun beating down on him, he thought he would quickly grow tired of the task at hand, but instead he became frustrated with his circumstances—the collapsed bridge, the world in general. After the fifth car, he was cursing under his breath.

After the sixth, he was kicking out the windows and punching off the rear-view mirrors before letting it fall into the abyss.

To find more cars, he walked to a housing development on the other side of the golf course.

"Stupid piece of shit," he said as the next one fell alongside the previous ones.

He alternated the cars going off from the right and left so they braced against each other instead of tumbling away from the pile he was trying to make.

At one time, each car had been part of Detroit's lifeblood. Men and women had spent their entire lives sitting in factories larger than the average person could comprehend, assembling each piece until it was ready to be shipped around the country. Now, they served no better purpose than to be pushed into a crevice. How long would the cars' skeletons remain in a pile? The paint and shine would be gone within a year or two. The plastic would still look fairly new by the time the metal had rusted holes throughout. A million years from now, after all the world's tombstones were broken and gone, after the famous monuments were all dust, piles of rubber tires would still be sitting in the gap where the bridge used to stretch.

It was only then, as he thought about the history of each thing he was dropping into the gap, that his anger faded and exhaustion took its place. Being upset was silly, he realized as he wiped sweat away from his eyes, because he was only there due to the choices he had made. He didn't have to drive north. He didn't have to drive in the tank. The decisions he made had gotten him here. Nothing else.

He walked all the way back to the housing development and got another car.

It was nighttime when he finally finished. The stack was by no means a nicely organized set of cubes. One of the cars had settled onto its side. Another had landed ass up. But it would work.

A fear lingered that, as soon as the tank rolled onto the makeshift plug in the bridge, one of the cars would shift positions and the entire stack would crumble away, taking his tank down with it. But with the stars overhead and his eyelids heavy, all he wanted was to get to the other side and go to sleep.

This time he did gun the engine as fast as it would go. The longer he took to get the tank across, the more he tempted the cars to crumble or shift. With a great howl, the tank raced up the bridge. The pile of cars gave a loud whine, but held, and his tank made it over the gap to the other side.

One of his last thoughts that night was how curious it was that he never thought about turning around when he saw the broken bridge. Yes, it was the only way to keep heading along the coast, but he could have turned around and backtracked until he got to another route that would get him north.

But his very last thought, as it always was, was of his son. He thought about Galen crossing those bridges with him. He thought about his boy sleeping under the stars with him. Just as quickly, his thoughts turned and he was thinking of his son on fire. His son's flesh had melted away while he was still alive. It had blistered and boiled, then dripped off his bones until he was a charred mass of skeleton and ash.

The thought stayed with him in his nightmares, and each time he woke up, it was to the sound of his own screams and cries.

Chapter 9

As Katherine twitched in her sleep, Jeffrey stared out the open window at the night sky and the city lights in the distance. The city's skyline was a reminder of the magnificent achievements mankind was capable of crafting. He liked to think Tokyo's brilliant array of lights would remain on even after its inhabitants were gone. Maybe all of the gaudy lights and sounds coming out of Las Vegas would still be on display after the final resident disappeared from the earth. Fewer and fewer people were around to see these things, just as there were fewer people to see the Philadelphia skyline each night. One day, not long in the future, the light show would be for one person only, and then, soon afterward, for no one at all.

From where his head rested on his pillow he could see the empty Lee house, the still-occupied Peluso house, and part of the formerly abandoned Ramirez home, which was now being used by a nice family from Vermont.

A conversation was taking place outside. Jeffrey looked over at the clock. 3 A.M. Long gone were the days when the youth of the world stayed out late at house parties and cops had to be called to issue warnings.

The voices he heard belonged to a man and a woman. The conversation only ended after a car door opened and closed. He could guess what was happening: another couple was packing their car with bags for the trip south. Another house would be empty when he woke up the next morning.

As the car left the neighborhood, a little flicker of

light caught Jeffrey's eye. The flickering seemed like nothing more than a night-light to keep children from being scared in the dark. It was playful, though, lively and energetic. What an odd light for a car to make, he thought. But the light remained even as the car's engine faded in the distance.

Something wasn't right. The light kept moving, kept growing. Still moving, still flickering.

Half confused, half fascinated, he propped himself up on one elbow. The light continued to dance. An alarm started in the back of his head. As the light continued moving, he got out of bed, walked down the hallway to the front door, and then outside, his bare feet cold on the ground.

The Meursault house, Jeffrey and Katherine's next-door neighbor, was in flames. A single car was stopped at the end of the street, waiting there as if to make sure the few prized possessions they couldn't squeeze into their car would be successfully burned to the ground. The car's taillights, two little red beacons, looked like evil eyes staring at him. Then the car turned the corner and the lights disappeared. The Meursaults were gone.

"Son of a bitch," he muttered. He wanted to get in his car and chase them down. He would drag Dave Meursault back to the burning house and ask the man how he could endanger another family like that; the wind could easily carry the fire to Jeffrey's house.

These thoughts took less than a second to process. Then he was running. Sprinting.

The Meursault's house was already engulfed in flames. But still, oddly, it was quiet. *Those sons of bitches disconnected their smoke detectors!*

The entire house was on fire now. Black smoke,

even darker than the night sky, rose into the air. The city and its lights were gone, hidden behind the smoke monster growing out of his neighbor's house.

Back inside his home, he yelled, "Fire."

Katherine was sitting upright, rubbing the sleep out of her eyes.

"Fire," he yelled again, even though he was only ten feet away from her this time.

She jumped off the bed. "What happened?" she asked as she packed a small bag with their wallets, some extra money, and the car keys.

It dawned on him that she might be thinking it was their house that was on fire instead of their neighbor's, but he liked her responsiveness. And, with the wind blowing, it easily could be their house next.

"I'm getting Galen," he said. "Get outside and call the fire department."

Hopefully, someone would take the call and arrive to put the fire out. If they didn't, Jeffrey knew his house would be burning in a matter of minutes.

Without saying another word, Katherine was out of the room and gone. Already, smoke was making its way into their home from next door. Jeffrey ran down the hall, scooped his son out of bed, and threw him into the wheelchair. He would apologize later for letting Galen's head hit the corner of the bedpost, but for now he just wanted to get his son out of the house as quickly as possible.

He coughed. Smoke was passing into every open room. His eyes were watering.

There was an impossible amount of smoke. His house must be on fire too. He couldn't control his coughing now. As he pushed Galen's wheelchair down the hall, he ran into a doorway because he couldn't keep his eyes open. The lights were on, but he could only look down and see his feet. Everything else was clouded with black smoke. The picture frames at the end of the hallway were gone, vanished behind the dark haze. The attic door was gone. Even the hallway lights. More coughing.

It was his habit of taking Galen out to the porch every evening—ten paces, turn left, five more paces, up one step at the door, then fresh air!—that got him out to safety. Even with his eyes closed he could make the journey. He passed the wheelchair over to Katherine before falling over with hacking coughs. It seemed like tar or sludge would eventually come out of his throat, but no matter how much he coughed nothing appeared.

Surprisingly, fire trucks were coming down the street. He was shocked at their responsiveness considering it was a hobby for the volunteers these days, and they had grown tired of putting out migration-fires.

One of the firemen asked Katherine if the fire was another case of flee-and-burn, and she said it was.

"Goddamn Meursaults," Jeffrey said.

The hoses had already begun spraying water all over the house. The roof collapsed. A minute later one of the walls caved in.

"Damn it," Jeffrey yelled, running his fingers through Galen's hair. "We lived next to them for ten years, and this is what they do at the end? I don't care if they head south early, but why sneak away in the middle of the night like criminals?" Then he yelled, "And why the hell would you burn your house down?"

Some of their other neighbors were standing on their front porches to see what was happening.

“There are a hundred nicer houses all around us,” Katherine said. “It didn’t have anything to do with their home; it’s the people. You can’t trust anyone to think about anything other than themselves.”

The other neighbors went back to bed. Some of them would also leave in the upcoming days. Some already knew when they were going to sneak away and were simply counting down the days. Others didn’t know they were going to abandon the city until something like this happened and they saw how you might as well leave sooner rather than later if you were surrounded by people who would do something like this.

**

The shopping center’s parking lot had room for two hundred vehicles. Other than a group of abandoned cars parked at the far end of the center, the entire area was vacant. Jeffrey was only there because a used bookstore caught his eye. Like a snotty businessman driving his luxury sports car, he parked the tank so it took up four spots.

A black and white house cat, abandoned long ago, was at the end of the line of stores, chasing a mouse or a chipmunk in circles around the concrete. Every time the cat caught up to the rodent, it batted at it and smacked it across the pavement until the little creature conceded defeat. Each time the mouse gave up, however, the cat lost interest in the game just long enough for its adversary to regain hope and attempt another dash for safety. Only then would the cat chase it again. The cat was a complete asshole.

The bookstore was between a beauty salon and drug store. Further down the line were a coffee shop, a discount clothing store, and a grocery store. Inside the bookstore, he turned and looked out the front window instead of immediately looking through the aisles in search of something interesting to read. The glass gave a clear view of the traffic that would have been coming into and out of the shopping center back when people were around.

It was then, right as he was about to start looking for which books he would take, that he saw a man crossing the parking lot.

The man appeared from the grocery store, saw the tank, then stopped to look around for where the tank's driver might be. Maybe, too, the man was scanning for other new vehicles in the area, or was wondering what purpose the tank could have in the remote strip mall. For a minute, the man looked all around him as though he might be on a hidden camera show. Why else would a tank not be there one minute and then be there the next? Then, as if seeing a woman for the first time after having served a long prison sentence, the man put the groceries down on the concrete and started walking, almost running, directly toward the tank.

Jeffrey watched, amused, before realizing what was happening. The man's single-minded focus on the machine caused a tiny thought to form in Jeffrey's head. The thought confused him at first because of how alien it was to the rest of his trip. Once formed, though, he stared in shock.

He was going to be robbed of his tank.

He threw the café door open. He was sprinting. It was obvious from both men's hobbled runs that neither of them had participated in track and field in a very, very long time. Jeffrey got to the thief right as he was pulling himself up on top of the tread.

"Stop," Jeffrey said, taking hold of the man's ankle as he climbed up the giant vehicle.

But instead of giving up the prize in front of him, the man shook his foot free before kicking it into Jeffrey's mouth. Jeffrey crashed to the ground. The man was standing atop the tank's tread, looking at the hatch to see how it opened.

Jeffrey was back on his feet, blood trickling from his mouth. The man turned and saw Jeffrey' extended arms and tried to stomp them away.

"You son of a bitch," Jeffrey growled.

He took one giant step forward before jumping to grab hold of any part of the thief he could cling to. If he missed, the man could move away and step inside the hatch. Once there, if he knew how, he could lock the hatch door from the inside. No matter how long Jeffrey rode on top of the tank, swearing at him, the new driver could keep going south until he ran out of gas. Maybe the thief would never open the hatch door. Maybe he would be content to drive south until he couldn't go any further, then simply die inside the machine that had once more given him hope. If that happened, Jeffrey would be back where he started, minus the tank.

But he didn't miss. His arms wrapped around one of the thief's legs, and as Jeffrey yanked with all of his might, the man came flying off the side of the metal hull and crashed hard against the concrete below.

He didn't get to ask why the man was doing what he was doing. He didn't even get to ask where this person was from or if anyone else was nearby. After hitting the ground, the thief took one disoriented swing toward Jeffrey, but by then Jeffrey was too mad to do anything except completely break the robber. He knelt on top of the thief, choking the man with one hand and punching him in the face with the other. The body underneath him growled and flailed.

"I need that tank," the thief said, almost begging, not even bothering to look at Jeffrey if it meant taking his eyes off the beautiful armored machine in front of him. One of the man's eyes was already swollen shut. His nose was crooked, pointing toward his shoulder instead of down toward his mouth. "I need that tank," he said again and again.

What made Jeffrey angrier than being kicked in the mouth was that this man had no concern for why Jeffrey had been here in the first place. What if he had been trying to get north to save his family? Without the tank, they would starve while this man rode south without any thought about their lives. What if the tank was traveling to some forgotten lab where a scientist had finally discovered a cure for the Blocks? Instead of saving all of humanity, the cure would go unused and be lost. The man didn't care about anything other than himself. And for that reason, under Jeffrey's weight, he became the men who had started the fire at the stadium. He was every man who had protested against the Blocks. He was Katherine leaving Galen at the stadium. He was the skeleton riling up fear each night. He was the lit match. He was every person who had burned their house down. He was every punch line to every Block joke.

That was what made Jeffrey keep hitting the thief, even after he had stopped resisting. One of his knuckles cracked after hitting the side of the man's skull. A flash of pain seared through Jeffrey's wrist, but instead of stopping the punishment, he merely switched hands. When that hand began to throb, he began slamming the thief's face into the pavement.

Looking back, he wasn't sure how soon after he had started hitting the thief that the man had given up resisting. By the time Jeffrey collected himself, the newcomer was unconscious on the pavement. Jeffrey was gasping for breath. His chest was heaving up and down as he shook in rage.

Even after he stood up, he was growling. The thief might be dead, yet Jeffrey still wasn't satisfied. This man had torched his boy. This man had taken everything away from him.

Part of Jeffrey wanted to break the man's arms and legs, just on the chance he was still alive, so if he woke up he would be able to do nothing except sit under the sky and think about what he had done until he died. He thought about tying the man's body across the top of the tank so everywhere he went, people would know to leave him alone. The man gave a pitiful gurgle on his own blood, but it could have been nothing more than the last breath escaping the body. Jeffrey was still shaking uncontrollably.

If someone else appeared, even if they weren't a robber, Jeffrey would kill that man too. He thought of Katherine driving his boy to the stadium. He thought of strangers telling her everything would be all right before dragging Galen out of the backseat and carrying him into the giant structure. At that moment, he would kill anyone he could get his hands on. He would kill them in front of their crying wives and children just as they had surely shrugged as Galen's flesh melted into the stadium seats.

To calm himself, he left the body on the ground and paced the aisles of the bookstore. He took *The Count of Monte Cristo*, *Great Expectations*, and *Rose Madder* because he wanted stories of revenge and anger.

Next, he walked to the grocery store. As soon as he stepped inside, even without seeing them, he could hear snakes sliding across the floor and rats scurrying for cover. The cat had been playing games with the rodent because it had as much food as it could ever want. Birds were squawking from the ceiling beams. Insects, maybe locusts, were chirping from every hidden recess. The supermarket had developed its own ecosystem.

Jeffrey looked down to the end of the cereal aisle. A pack or a swarm or whatever they were called of various kinds of snakes was intertwined like loose threads. Various animals' shit covered every patch of the formerly glossy floor. There was even a bald eagle in the one corner of the ice cream section, eyeing the wildlife two stories below. When it turned and looked at the newcomer, Jeffrey slowly backed out of the store.

The man, bloody and broken, probably dead, was still at front of the tank. Jeffrey knew from the way he had come out of the grocery store alone and by the way he ran toward the tank without a second thought, that he had probably been by himself for a long time. The man's face looked like a grotesque impression of cheese dropped in boiling water. Dried red and black bits were caked around both nostrils and both eyes. One eye was swollen completely shut. The other was purple and half closed. One eyebrow looked like it was missing, only to be replaced with black pus and blood. Flies were already landing on the man.

"Just kill me," the thief mumbled, his eyes unable to open. The man offered sounds of what would have been crying if he could breath normally. "Please, just kill me," the man sobbed.

"I'm going to leave you here," Jeffrey said. "If you can get up and walk away, fine. If you stay here and die, that's fine too. But I want to tell you something first, and I want you to listen, to truly hear what I'm saying. Your decisions are the reason you are here in this condition. It's not my fault. It's not the fault of anyone else who left already to go south. Just you."

The man didn't move as Jeffrey climbed back into the tank. Probably, he would never move from that spot.

The tank rumbled away from the shopping center and began heading north again.

Chapter 10

The skeleton and his adversary shared one of the few moments of silence that sometimes occurred between the barking and cynical laughter. Jeffrey was sure it was all scripted by the show's producer to add more tension, to make it seem like the two men were afraid of what they would do if either of them argued one second longer. Katherine didn't believe him; she saw the two men yelling and knew if she ever argued that way it would be because something made her snap, and that kind of emotion, that kind of outrage, was too serious to fake.

"And how are all these Blocks going to magically get transported to Washington? Are we going to find every spare bus in the city and have a caravan of thousands of helpless people trailing behind us? What happens when the first bus breaks down and obstructs the path for the other thousand buses? Is everyone else supposed to wait for them?"

The editorial in that week's paper had offered the same sentiment: it was unfair for the normal people in Philadelphia to be burdened with getting all of the Blocks to Washington. The only people who felt this way, Jeffrey believed, were the ones that didn't have Block relatives or, if they once had, had already dropped them off at a Block shelter. If you didn't have anyone to take care of, it was easy to forget the world was full of people less fortunate than you. There would always be people who forgot about the world around them and focused solely on their own survival. What bothered Jeffrey was that these people now had an organized voice.

Each time he heard these things, he wanted to punch a hole in the wall.

It didn't help the city's growing panic that a lot of the families sneaking away in the middle of the night were leaving behind additional Blocks—a Block or two who would be added to all the others that everyone would be responsible for. Each day that went by meant more Blocks taking up space at the Block group centers. The converted high school gymnasiums, homeless shelters, and rec centers were spread throughout the city.

And each day, another regular person died of old age or sickness. The Blocks had become the city's silent majority. Projections charted that the city's population, if nothing changed ten years from now, would consist of ninety percent Blocks and only ten percent normal people. No one wanted to be one of those remaining few, to be responsible, on average, for nine bodies that couldn't do anything for themselves.

The skeleton and the man across from him were still talking: "I can't believe how reckless you would be with everyone's lives if this relocation was up to you."

"I'd rather be reckless than scared and inconsiderate."

"What you are is fat."

That was when the skeleton's opponent—big-boned, not fat—lunged over the table separating them and tried to get in as many good shots as time would allow, before the producers and camera crew pulled him off.

Jeffrey groaned before making the TV go dark. Katherine got up and read in silence while Jeffrey sat outside with their son.

"Quiet night," he said once Galen was positioned on

the porch to face the street. “In a couple of days, the birds will have the entire place to themselves.” He took a sip of beer before adding, “That would be something to see.”

He watched Galen’s breathing. It was his favorite thing in the world. Always relaxed, each breath steady. Jeffrey was surrounded by men and women who were worried about transitioning to a new city, to a new phase in their lives, but here was his son, unflappable, always at ease, always at peace with the world.

Down the street, a van was pulling into the Sparts’ driveway. Their house had been vacant for two years. The one-time semi-celebrities of the neighborhood, famous for killing a home-invader and then daring the police to charge them with something, were one of the first families to disappear after the population started to decline. It was rumored the cops didn’t like being called out the way they had, and had made it look like the Sparts relocated south, when in fact they were at the bottom of the Delaware River.

It was common, as people vanished to go south, for old grudges to be settled by simply making people disappear. In a world where your neighbors left without saying goodbye, it was easy to believe your best friend might be capable of the same thing. But instead of getting a postcard from them once they had arrived in Texas or Florida, their dead bodies were eventually found. People who disappeared and were assumed to have relocated were found in landfills and in the woods with bullets in their heads.

Nowhere was this more common than in Russia. The oldest living Russians still remembered the days of Stalin and knew right away what was happening. They had been alive when millions of Russians disappeared over the span of a decade. They also knew, as the adage warns us, that history always repeats itself.

It wasn't until bodies—people who were thought to have relocated to Greece or Turkey—were found, rotting in Moscow landfills, that a new generation of Russians began to understand the way the world worked. The Great De-evolution signaled the perfect way to pay back grudges that had been thought forgotten. Wave after wave of Russians came to their ends through these disappearances. Even Stalin would have been proud of the extent of the vanishings and the way they were carried out.

When a third of the Russian president's cabinet members disappeared one night—the third of the room that had disagreed with his latest budget proposal—they were said to have all decided, on the same night, to pack up and head toward the Caspian Sea. Most of their bodies, however, were found in a shallow ditch just outside the city limits a week later. When his first wife disappeared, everyone was told she must have gone to their luxury home in India. Her fingers turned up in a field outside Moscow. Her feet were found almost two hundred miles away in Kovrov. The rest of her was never found.

The next time Jeffrey went to take a sip of beer, the can was empty. Katherine seemed to be in his head because she appeared with a new can, the tab already pulled. She didn't say anything before re-entering the house, empty can in hand.

When she was gone, he watched a family of four get out of the van in the Sparts' driveway. All four people, two men and two women, looked to be around his age. The Sparts' old home was now their home. Maybe they were the last vestiges from New York or Boston. Maybe even Canada. It didn't matter if these four people had been bank robbers, cannibals, or neurosurgeons; everyone had a fresh start when they moved to a new city; they were just more people traveling south with everyone else. Maybe they would leave with everyone else for Washington, or maybe they would enjoy the empty city after it was vacated, the same way they had stayed in whichever previous city they had just come from. Maybe there was something cathartic about being in a city immediately after everyone else had left.

Each of the newcomers had a single suitcase and backpack that they carried into the house. As he watched them, Jeffrey went to take another sip of beer, but this one had somehow completely vanished into his mouth as well.

"I'll be right back," he told Galen. "Hold the fort down."

He carried the empty can back inside. There were only bottles left. He searched the drawer for the bottle opener, but couldn't find the place where Katherine kept it. Like he did in college, he put the edge of the bottle against the countertop and smacked the top so the cap broke off. Normally he would get in trouble for that. Today, he knew it didn't matter because the house would be empty soon. The indentations would stay behind as one of the million small reminders that a family had been there, had laughed and cried, had lived and loved.

Right at that moment, a voice, faint in the distance, could be heard to say, "I got his arms. You grab his legs." Jeffrey listened for the TV, but there was only silence. Katherine was still upstairs reading. Even so, it didn't register with him exactly where the words could have come from. He even paused for a moment, just long enough to hold his step and listen for more sounds.

That was when he heard giggling. But it wasn't coming from their TV. It was coming from outside. From his porch. He darted toward the screen door.

Galen was gone.

The two chairs were still there, exactly where they

had been, but his son was gone. Something was wrong; Blocks didn't just get up and walk away. Katherine was still inside. Something was wrong. His boy was gone.

God help me, he thought.

A small movement caught the corner of his eye.

In the fading light of dusk, he saw three figures, trying their best to remain still, huddled by a telephone pole. The three of them held a long, slender object in their arms. They appeared to be young men, maybe just slightly older than Galen, but in the fading light he couldn't be sure. They stared at him without moving until they were sure he saw them. As soon as Jeffrey started toward them, one of them yelled, "Shit!" and the three took off.

The thing they had been carrying—Galen—was dropped where they stood. His son fell three feet before hitting the ground. His poor boy couldn't do so much as put his arms out to brace for the fall, and Jeffrey watched as his son's face smacked the earth. In any other circumstance, Jeffrey would have raced to his boy's side and made sure he wasn't hurt. This time, though, he raced after the three kidnappers.

As he gave chase, he realized he was chasing three young men who should either be studying for finals or resting after a long day's work. But, without a reason to go to college, these kids, who all looked like they might have been born around the same time the Blocks started appearing, resented that their lives were pointless in the changing world. Maybe the boys thought Blocks like Galen would get them sick. Or perhaps it was just juvenile fun to kidnap someone who couldn't talk or move, the same way it had been fun for Jeffrey to spray-paint billboards or toilet paper people's houses when he was their age.

Didn't these stupid kids know they were the lucky

ones? They could move and talk and live their lives. His son couldn't do any of those things. If anyone had a right to resent the world, it was his son. And yet the boy was a quiet Buddha to the world's chaos.

As he gave chase, he wondered what the boys had planned on doing with his son. There had been a story on the news three days earlier about a group of young men who had been found in an abandoned house torturing a Block. When the cops busted in, one of the young men had been holding a lighter to the Block's ear just to watch it burn. The Block had sat there, unfazed, unflinching, and would have continued sitting there until he was dead or the kids lost interest in him. A year earlier, the Block Butcher had finally been caught and arrested in San Francisco. The Butcher was thought to have tortured and killed more than one hundred Blocks in California. Some reports said he had eaten parts of his victims to see if Block flesh tasted like regular people.

It was also possible they merely wanted to move Galen to a porch further down the street. How funny it would be for them to watch Jeffrey's expression as he went outside, saw his son was missing, only to see him sitting on a porch two houses down the road. The kids would be howling with laughter. Or maybe they would think it hilarious to dress Galen in weird clothes before delivering him back to the very spot where they stole him.

Without knowing their intentions, Jeffrey assumed the worst.

Still running, he wanted to kill anyone who would harm his boy. "You motherfuckers," Jeffrey yelled as he ran.

Two of the three young men seemed to appreciate the trouble they were in. The third one burst out laughing after hearing Jeffrey's threat. When Jeffrey yelled at them a second time, the three kidnappers darted in different directions. One of them seemed defeated just by hearing the threats and began looking behind him to see how fast Jeffrey was closing in on him rather than looking for where he could escape to.

Jeffrey wasn't sure if he yelled, "I'm going to kill you," or if he merely thought it, but the boy cried out and started running in a different direction again. The young man, gasping for breath, was barely jogging anymore, looking absolutely petrified to have a fifty year-old man running down the street after him. As far as Jeffrey was concerned, the other two kids were gone. The one remaining thief was only ten feet ahead now.

The young man turned once again in the hope that Jeffrey was too tired to keep up the chase. Instead, Jeffrey was only five feet behind him now. The kid whimpered as he gave a hobbled jog forward. At the Matthews' lawn, he was almost able to reach out and grab the kid's shirt. When they got to the Garcias' old lawn, the kidnapper started zigzagging, a desperate last ditch attempt to get away. But this only lasted for another ten seconds and then the boy was done. Right before Jeffrey was able to grab him, he turned to face his punishment head on.

Instead of tackling the kid to the ground, Jeffrey drove his foot into the kidnapper's stomach as hard as he could, as if stomping forward, a simple push-kick taught years earlier in basic training. With the kidnapper barely moving and with Jeffrey having a running start, the force of his kick was incredible. The boy flew backward through the Caseys' front yard before coming to a rest in the fetal position. As Jeffrey stood over the young man, he saw the kid gagging to get more oxygen. A goat could have appeared and offered noises that made more sense.

Jeffrey didn't bother asking the kid why he had

tried to steal Galen. He simply ran the ten feet to where the boy was huddled on the grass and soccer kicked him as hard as he could, square across his face. The young man was motionless and quiet. There was no giant pool of blood the way there always was in movies. There weren't sirens approaching from the distance. There wasn't even a scream from a concerned neighbor. In that moment, alone, the city might as well have already been abandoned.

"You stupid asshole," Jeffrey said. "Don't ever touch my son."

God help the young thief if Jeffrey happened to be holding a knife or a gun at that exact instant. The amount of pain and blood on display would have been astounding. Even with just his bare hands, he thought about tearing at the kidnapper's face until his eyes and lips were gone. He thought about using a sharp rock to scalp the defeated mess beneath him. Anything he could think of to hurt this person in front of him, he would have relished it.

Instead, he merely turned and started back for home. As he turned the corner at Glebe Road, he looked back one more time. The kid was still motionless, still alone. It was no loss if the body just sank into the ground without any fanfare.

"Piece of shit," Jeffrey muttered as he walked back home. "He's a living, breathing person," he said, crying. "He's my son. Why would someone want to harm my boy? Why would anyone want to harm anyone else?"

No one was around to answer his questions. He was sobbing now. In that moment, if he saw the other thieves he would do his best to kill them too. Right then, as mad as he was, he would kill just about anyone except his family.

"Touch my son and you're dead!" he yelled.

He noticed then that he was in front of the Sparts'

house. The four newcomers were watching him from the living room window of their newly inherited house as he stalked down the road. Quite the neighborhood welcome. They were probably scared shitless at what they could only assume, on their first night in the neighborhood, was a nightly occurrence. He wouldn't be surprised if the van was gone when the sun came back up.

His heart stopped when he got to his driveway: Galen was gone!

The other two guys must have circled back for his boy. He looked up and down the street for any sign of his son. Maybe there had been more than the three thieves he saw originally, and the kids he chased off had merely served as a distraction. A band of deviants would spend the night torturing Galen until the poor boy was dead. His son would be all alone in the cold, probably out in the middle of a forest, maybe in an abandoned basement, as a group of kids, not much older than the one Jeffrey had just caught, took turns burning him with their lighters, pissing on him, breaking his fingers, and laughing the entire time because nothing they did would elicit a response.

Katherine came to the front door then. Her hands were on her hips the way she held them when she disapproved of something.

"Did you see where they took him?" he yelled at her from the edge of the street.

"What is going on out here?"

"Our son! Galen. Where did they take him?"

She stomped her foot on the ground. "I," she said, an accent appearing out of nowhere, part Midwest, part English. "I took our son back inside because his father was nowhere to be found."

"They were going to light him on fire."

He was almost crazed now, confused. Looking back, he thought how poorly he performed when his family needed him to be calm.

Katherine asked how their son ended up in the grass.

"Some kids," he said. "Some random pieces of shit were going to kidnap Galen and torture him."

"Kids?" Her voice emphasized skepticism.

"You know what I mean. Guys. A couple of young guys just a little older than Galen."

"Was he hurt?"

"You're the one who took him inside," he said.

"He seemed fine," she said, still looking confused about the whole thing and why her son had been sitting on the ground by a telephone pole.

"Why aren't you more upset?"

"I don't understand what happened."

Maybe on the news the next day the anchorman would talk about a kid who had been stomped to death and then Katherine would realize how serious things had been. He walked past her without saying anything else, disappeared into the house, while she remained standing on the porch. The first thing he did, before washing the blood from his hands, before looking at himself in the mirror to see if he looked like a crazed maniac, was go to his son's room. And there Galen was, back in his wheelchair.

"It's OK," he said as he scooped his son up in his arms and transferred him into bed.

Katherine was in the doorway saying something. He

didn't hear what she said, and when he looked up the next time she was gone.

In the old days, before the Blocks appeared and people slowly started moving south, the police would have arrived at his door, handcuffed him, and taken him to the station for processing. The parents of the boy he had kicked would have sued him for everything he was worth, even though he was only protecting his son. He could even imagine himself yelling, "But they were hurting my boy!" as the cops handcuffed him and put him in the backseat of their cruiser. Now, though, even if they did receive a call that a fight had taken place down the street and someone was in critical condition, the police would ask what it was they were expected to do, seeing as how the city's population was getting ready to head south.

There was no use in arresting people for fighting. There was no use in arresting people for almost anything these days. Unless you were the Block Butcher and went around killing people just for kicks, you shouldn't expect to be arrested. Speeders had no fear of getting tickets. You could smoke whatever you wanted in front of the cops and they would shrug. You were free to piss right in front of a cop car and no one would do anything about it.

"Everything will be all right," he told Galen again. "I won't let them hurt you." He held his son's head in his arms. He stayed like that, Galen resting against him, the way he had when his son was just a baby, until it was completely dark out and Jeffrey's eyes refused to stay open. The bedroom light was already off and Katherine asleep when he got upstairs.

It wasn't until his son's eyes randomly closed that Jeffrey's temper finally subsided and he too could think about sleep.

**

He had the option of turning off of 95 and heading more directly north, but chose instead to stay on the course that kept him near the water.

He never thought about going west. Going inland would only leave him feeling lost. If he drove the tank into one of the national parks, he would become overwhelmed with options. Should he keep going west or should he keep north? Should he stop and enjoy the wilderness, or should he see where each winding road led? He would die in the forests, far from anything he knew. Staying in line with the ocean kept him next to something familiar.

Just before noon, he stopped the tank and looked out across the water at an island in the distance. With the water between him and the land, he couldn't tell if it was a mile away or ten miles away. It looked deceptively close, but he knew if he tried to swim there he would never make it. There was no smoke coming from the island, no sign that it was inhabited.

Years earlier, the parcel of land had been taken over by a group of people who didn't want anything to do with Blocks, which was ironic since it was called Block Island. Just east of Montauk, the island became their private Block-free settlement. Anyone was welcome as long as they didn't bring a victim of the Great De-evolution with them. Not long after it was established, the anti-Block settlement stopped communicating with the rest of the world, and no one was sure if they simply chose not to interact with others, or if they had all died.

On the edge of the mainland, a stack of bodies was piled on the side of the road. Most still had remnants of rotted, decomposing flesh, but some were nothing more than bleach-white bone. A billboard read, 'Block Island Welcomes You.' Only now, it also had the spray-painted words, 'But not your Blocks.'

The message was clear to anyone struggling to make their way south: you could stop traveling, stop struggling to fix your flat tires each day, stop worrying. All you had to do was leave your quiet brother or sister, your motionless son or daughter, on the side of the road. And then your worries could go away.

He tried to think of a set of circumstances where his situation could get so bad he might consider ditching Galen before entering their settlement. Even faced with death, faced with struggling to live, eventually dying on the side of the road with no one but his son, he would rather die a hundred times in a hundred different places than go to the settlement just once if it meant betraying his boy.

He left the bodies there, rotting, food for maggots and flies. It was someone else's shame that they were there, not his.

The tank continued on.

It only took an hour on Highway 1 before he regretted getting off 95. The tank approached a giant tree in the road, and it was obvious the machine would not be able to make it over the obstacle. The road-blocked, isolated stretch of highway made him think of old TV shows in which someone got out of their car only to get ambushed by men waiting in the tree line. There was no sign of human life here, though, so he climbed down from the tank to assess the giant tree in his path.

Instead of running into a band of criminals, Jeffrey was greeted by an elderly man. And instead of looking into the barrel of a gun, the person staring at him offered a smile and waved hello. The little, grey-haired man showed no concern that a tank had appeared, a tank that could feasibly destroy his home in seconds, there was only pleasure at seeing another person. That was what being alone for too long did to you.

Without even bothering to close his front door, the man began shuffling toward Jeffrey. He would plant his cane into the ground, make sure it was steady, then scuttle a leg forward. His back was so hunched over he appeared to be half the size of a normal person.

“Fancy meeting you here!” the old man called out.

“How’s it going?” Jeffrey said, offering his arm for the old man to take hold of.

“It’s been a long time since someone has come through these parts.”

“How long?”

“I reckon five years. Probably longer.”

“You’ve been here by yourself the entire time?”

The old man shook his head. “Not many people take these roads anymore when they can shoot down 95 to get south.”

“There isn’t much of that anymore either,” Jeffrey said. “I only saw one small group, just south of New York. No one else.”

“So why are you in these parts then, young man?”

“I wanted to stay near the water.”

“A man after my own heart. I keep my windows open so I can smell the salt water all day.”

Jeffrey said, “I’ll help you over to the beach if you want to go.”

The old man chuckled, maybe even blushed.

Jeffrey added, “It would be my good deed for the day.”

“I don’t remember the last time I did a good deed.”

“I doubt many people do.”

“That’s the problem with the world,” the old man said.

“The problem with the world is the Blocks can’t have children and we’re all dying out.”

“Well,” the old man chuckled, “there’s that too. I thank you for the offer, but you save your good deed for someone else. Don’t waste it on this silly old man.”

“It doesn’t have to be a one time deal. I can help someone else tomorrow.”

“Maybe,” the old man said, as if suddenly realizing that was possible. “Maybe,” he said again.

“Why are you here by yourself?”

“I’m not really sure.”

“You don’t know how you ended up here alone?”

“Don’t talk to me like that. I’m old, but I’m not stupid. My family were some of the first people to head south. I stayed here because one of my friends needed my help. He got sick so I took care of him while the next caravan was leaving. Eventually, he got better and headed south too, but I stayed.”

“But why?”

“It was all I knew by that time. I got so used to seeing the people I know leave, one by one, that it became the norm. I wasn’t even sad when my friend went south because I’d already seen my family leave—my parents, my wife, my daughter, my other friends. Going south and seeing them again would have felt stranger than staying in the place I knew."

Jeffrey asked what the man did all day. Surely, he would have some great insight to the world after turning the beach town into a giant meditation chamber for himself.

"Think about my mistakes, mostly," the old man said, then looked carefully at Jeffrey for a moment before continuing. "I killed a man once. I still don't even know why, except I was young and dumb. I know it doesn't look like it, but this old man used to be something fierce. I was a two-time state champion wrestler in high school. Even got a full ride to wrestle in college. But I was an angry kid. Never had a reason to be, just was. After a night of drinking, I was walking back from dropping off my girlfriend at her dorm, and on my way back to my apartment this drunk guy started talking all sorts of nonsense. Didn't have a reason to other than he was drunk. Must have just been the unlucky circumstance of two angry people meeting. I swung at him, then got on top of him and hit him a couple more times. I knew I was in trouble when he shit himself. You don't do that just from going unconscious. I read in the paper the next day that a man was found beaten to death in an alley a couple of blocks away from the bar I'd been at. I kept expecting the cops to show up and arrest me, but no one did. And I never told anyone about it. Not even my wife. That's what I think about now, during all these days when I'm by myself. I think about why I did that in the first place, about the type of person I was to be able to do something like that. And I think about how my life would have been different if the police had come and arrested me. And of course I think about the life the man would have had if I hadn't killed him. Maybe he would have been the man to find a cure for the Blocks. Maybe he would have had a Block child of his own. Who knows? That's what I think about. Spent my entire life thinking about it. But no matter how much I think about it, I can never stop. Nothing will change what I did."

"You've never forgiven yourself for it?"

"I don't think I'm the one that can do the forgiving. The only person that can forgive me is already in the next life. I'll ask forgiveness when I see him again."

The man invited Jeffrey inside for a glass of iced tea or some food, but Jeffrey said he needed to be on his way. He watched as the old man, sorry to see the first visitor in five years leaving so soon, shuffled pitifully back to the front door of his house.

"And," the old man called out. "I think about the man's family and how angry they must have been. One day their son was alive and the next day he was dead. And for no better reason than some fight outside a bar. Life doesn't get much more unfair than that. I always thought I would know the man's family if I ran into them because they would be the angriest people on the face of the earth. I thought about searching them out and apologizing, but I knew that wouldn't do no good. That wouldn't help them, and it wouldn't take back what I did. I did a dumb thing, and because of that, one man's anger became an entire family's fury. That was when I stopped being an angry person. Because I realized, if you keep letting the anger of the world beat you down like that, if you let it eat away at you, before you know it, the entire world will be killing each other. It doesn't take back what I did, but it made me a better person."

The old man waved goodbye then, sorry to see his visitor leave so soon.

Jeffrey grumbled to himself. After all of that, the tree was still sitting there, still waiting to break his spirits.

Wanting to get away from the pitiful, old man, he decided to nudge the very edge of the tree with the tank and hopefully push it aside. He didn't look to see if the old man was watching him from the window. And when the tree was moved just slightly away from where it had been, he drove away without looking back.

His map showed a peninsula near by, the very edge of which was called Point Judith. The scene, when he arrived, was disappointing. He had hoped the peninsula would be wilderness, but it was a series of developments and non-stop beach homes. It was difficult to find an area where man hadn't littered the land with houses, most of which looked identical to one another.

Developers hadn't known what to do when the Great De-evolution started. All their lives, all they had known was how to build more and more houses. Even when there was a surplus of homes, they kept building because they couldn't think to do anything else. A year before the Great De-evolution started, you could find two or three homes for sale on every road in every city, and yet they still built new houses everywhere they could find undeveloped land. It was madness.

And it didn't stop just because the Great De-evolution signaled an end to man. Even when no new children were possible and the population kept shrinking, bulldozers were at work putting up new townhouses and single-family homes. Construction only stopped when the banks stopped lending money. That was the only way developers could control their nonsensical urge to build, build, build.

There's a townhouse complex just outside Boston that never sold a single unit because people started moving south. A chain of million-dollar luxury apartments was built in Dubai five years after the population started declining. In Budapest, construction on a new 200-unit apartment complex began even though people had started migrating south. Not to be outdone, a developer in Oregon tried to build a new 100-acre neighborhood of high-end homes. He only got as far as bull-dozing the entire forest where the new homes would be built before construction stopped due to too many men sneaking away to head south.

Point Judith was nowhere near those extremes, and the peninsula's tip offered a nice view. The focal point was a lighthouse positioned between the water and the houses.

He ended up staying four months.

During the days, he went for walks and read books. He took a blanket with him to the top of the lighthouse and spent one night doing nothing but staring up at the clear sky and at all the stars that were revealed once he was away from the city lights. The old man's words kept repeating in his head as he watched the night sky. He didn't want to be any of the people—the dead man, the murderer, the dead man's family—in the story that the man had told.

It was difficult not to imagine Galen there with him. Their talks on the front porch would magically become conversations in the lighthouse. He wondered if Galen would have been an angry person if he were normal. The old man had said he had no reason to be angry, yet he had been, so maybe Galen would have been the same way. Or maybe he would have been melancholy for no apparent reason.

Every once in a while, he found himself thinking about the stack of dead Blocks on the side of the road or of the living Block struggling to survive on the highway. He tried to forget these things, but they were always in the back of his mind along with how his son had died.

Often times, he would wake up in the middle of the

night, still in the top deck of the lighthouse, from crying in his sleep.

Three dogs roamed with him whenever he journeyed through the streets of abandoned homes. The animals always looked at him, but never approached. They were old enough to remember what it was like to have a human master, but the memories were from long ago and could no longer be fully trusted. Sometimes the dogs whined when they saw him, as if they too wished everything could go back to the way it had been. He didn't feed them because he didn't want them to learn to depend on him just to have him ride away in a couple of months.

He spent one day going into abandoned houses on a random street for no other reason than to see what kinds of things had been left behind and what things were missing. An empty wall with nails sticking out of the drywall used to hold family photos. Empty drawers had contained socks and underwear that were needed during the long journey ahead. It was all very depressing, and it wasn't long before the empty houses made him think of Galen and he wanted to go back to his reading.

Were the drawers in his own home empty? Had Katherine taken some of their family portraits with her when she left, or had they filled her with too much shame? He shook his head and groaned. His eyes burned. He tried to let the sound of the water help him forget what had happened to his son, but no matter how many times the waves crashed, he couldn't get the thought of Galen's burning body out of his mind. He rubbed at his eyes, but that didn't make anything better.

Chapter 11

The skeleton's opponent never returned after their on-air fight. It was assumed he had given up the debate and quietly moved south by himself. He hadn't provided much of the show's content, but even the skeleton noticed an element was missing without someone to sit across from him. No longer did he have to repeat himself as he was being interrupted, which had made his ideas seem even more taboo. No longer did he have someone to laugh at, which had made him appear to know truths about the world that no one else wanted to see. The only thing the producers could think of was to make him even more exaggerated. He went from making insinuations to direct accusations. The Blocks, he said, were making us all sick. Nothing was out of bounds. The Mayans had vanished after suffering from the Block disease. The first signs of the Block ailment had been discovered after researchers broke into King Tut's tomb.

Not even Katherine was interested in being scared by him anymore.

But, with the TV off, she did turn to Jeffrey and say, "I don't want to get sick."

"Bullshit," he said. He knew what she meant: she was afraid Galen might turn them into Blocks. He doubted she really believed that, but even saying it was bad enough. "You've been his mother for twenty years and he's never made you sick."

"Why am I always tired?"

"Because you worry all day. You listen to these

assholes on TV and you let them worry you until you're shaking. And I'm sick of it."

Her tears soaked into his shoulder before he could say another word. When the crying subsided, she said, "Remember when we were getting ready for our senior prom and I had that meltdown about my curfew? What happened to that girl? Where did she go?"

What was he supposed to say to that? The truth was, he often wondered the same thing—where had that girl gone? What had happened to the person who cried anytime she saw the sad faces of newborn kittens and puppies that were locked up in tiny pet store cages, none of them having a chance at a happy life? What had happened to the girl who dreamed of having a huge dining room so her entire family could visit for Thanksgiving? Just because the Great De-evolution signaled man's eventual end, it didn't mean that girl's dreams had to end too.

When he didn't speak, she added: "I'm afraid to spend another day in this city."

He asked what was wrong, but instead of answering, she only said they were stupid for not already having gone down to Washington. He asked what was so great about Washington.

"We never should have gotten married so young," she said.

That was when he got up from the sofa and went to see how Galen was doing. There was no point in arguing. There was no sense to asking another question only to hear another answer she didn't really mean.

Any time he was frustrated, he could look at his son and things would be better. There was never a trace of anxiety on Galen's face, never a hint of shame or embarrassment, not even when he needed to be changed into a new diaper. He was exclusively peaceful, as though touched by the hand of a monk that had learned all of the answers to life's questions. No matter what had happened that day, his son would have relaxed eyes and gentle breathing. Nothing was more heavenly.

As a teenager, Jeffrey had enjoyed fishing at the lake near his parent's house. The act of casting the line and reeling it in wasn't the relaxing part; it was the water that had soothed him, put him in a good state of mind. For years he had been sure there was nothing more tranquil and serene than that lake. Then Galen was born.

He used the quiet with his boy to calm his own nerves. As he sat there, looking at proof that it was possible to remain angelic through the end of the world, he wondered again what had happened to the woman he had fallen in love with. Where was the person who used to make him snort with laughter, who made him feel like he was the most loved man in the world? If only she could get the same sense of peace from seeing her son each day. If only all of the people protesting the Blocks, holding rallies against them, could see what Jeffrey saw.

It was then that he thought back to the Father's Day card she had written, as though from Galen, many years earlier.

"Please don't do this again," he had told her, looking down at her deliberately scribbled writing—meant to mimic what she thought Galen's hand-writing might be like.

Poor Galen had just stared at the wall while she wrote the card, signed it, and then, as if to authenticate it, rubbed the boy's index finger in ink so it left a smudged print next to his name. She had thought Jeffrey was angry with her, but he hadn't been upset with her at all, merely filled with anguish that his boy would never be able to write the card himself.

He couldn't tell her that was why he was upset, though, not after feeling like he had convinced her to have a child in the first place. And so he had never explained, never brought it up again. It was the first and last time she had ever acted as the go-between for Galen's love, one failed attempt at trying to be a messenger for the things their son might have said if he had a voice of his own. Was that also when she stopped changing the boy, when she stopped talking to him as though he might offer a reply? If only Jeffrey could have explained how sad it made him to have a voiceless child without making her feel like their son had been a mistake. But how do you do that when you were the one who wanted to cry because of the forged signature, when you were the one who had to bargain for the child in the first place? And so he never said anything.

That faked signature from their son had been the moment when he learned acts of love could be the most painful acts of all. Had she ever learned that lesson for herself, or was she overwhelmed with trying to learn all the other lessons life bombarded them with?

Maybe the woman he had fallen in love with hadn't vanished. Maybe she was just too busy trying to figure the world out for herself to keep being funny for Jeffrey each day.

**

He came upon a billboard that read "Leaving Rhode Island, Welcome to Massachusetts" and he laughed because he hadn't realized he was in Rhode Island until he was leaving it.

Everything he did, even something as simple as driving through the tiny state, made him miss his boy; Galen had never gotten a chance to see Rhode Island or any other part of New England. The tank passed by a large pond. If Galen was with him, they could have spent days watching bubbles rise to the surface while Jeffrey recounted what it was like to learn how to fish from Galen's grandfather.

He would never be able to take his boy to the lakes again. Galen would never be at his side as something caught their line. For the rest of time, Jeffrey would be by himself. What was the point of it all if that was how things were going to be?

He filled up on gasoline anytime he found working pumps. At one gas station, he even drove the dirt-covered tank through a carwash. The sprinklers and soap machines let loose with a barrage of bubbles as the tank crept through the washer. Suds came in through the long turret. He did it merely because Galen would have laughed at the absurdity of it all. But instead of making him smile, he found himself feeling like it was all pointless.

He picked up a stack of new books. He re-read *The Catcher in the Rye*. In high school, it had seemed hilarious and brilliant. Now, it seemed like the most depressing book he had ever read, and he wondered how it could have ever made him laugh. *The Stranger* had been one of his favorites in college. But now, the ending made him feel like there was no use in anything. He forced his way through *The English Patient* and *Flowers for Algernon* and *Disgrace*. Each book made him hate the world he lived in, made him want to go to sleep and never wake up again. If Galen were around, he could have read all the same stories aloud and they would have enjoyed them together. Without the boy there, every story was sadder than the last.

At the junction of 195 and 495 he headed south, one of the only brief times during his journey that he would let the tank face the equator. When he came to the shore again he got out and looked at the land separated by water. He had always wanted to see what Martha's Vineyard was like. There was almost no point in going if Galen couldn't see it with him, however.

Years earlier, there would have been hundreds of boats docked, each ready to take him across the water. Now, there were only three, and two of them looked like they would sink if he stepped inside them. If he did actually get out on the water, the current might take him out to sea.

How many people, without any sailing experience whatsoever, had chosen to venture forth on the ocean as a way to get south when they heard the roads were deteriorating? The tank wasn't fun to ride in, but at least it was simple to use. He knew better than to think he could just jump in a boat, get the sails working, and head safely in the right direction.

The seas were littered with the boats of people who hadn't known better. Some simply didn't have a clue about sailing but still managed to get out too far to be able to swim back to shore before the boat capsized or started drifting without purpose. Others would know enough to correctly get the sails rigged, but then wouldn't be able to navigate correctly and would let the current take them into the middle of the ocean where sharks looked up with grins. Still others would want to stay close to the shore, needing to see land to feel safe, until they ran aground, some of them drowning, others lucky enough to get back to dry land in some other random part of the country from where they had started.

He had two distinct fears. One was that the boat would go in the direction it wanted, not the direction he wanted it to go. This would happen because of wind or because he wouldn't know how to adjust the sails. A day later he would be so far out to sea that he wouldn't be able to spot land and would either drown trying to swim back to shore, or would die of dehydration in the middle of the Atlantic.

In Ireland, more dead bodies washed ashore each day as ghost ships were carried toward land. In Argentina, authorities stopped trying to identify where the ships and their dead passengers had come from. Along the coastline of South Africa, they didn't even bother to burn the ships or bury the dead. The bodies that arrived there were left to join the new cemeteries along the sand where it was easier for the elderly to dig graves for the Blocks.

His second fear was that he would be able to plot the boat's course without any problems—if he could figure out how to drive a tank, how hard could piloting a boat be?—but it would refuse to take him back to the mainland and he would be stuck on an island prison for the rest of his life—a Great De-evolution Napoleon.

He and Galen would never get out to see the Grand Canyon. There would never be a photo of him standing at the Golden Gate Bridge with his son. Here was a place, though, that he could get to and yet he was still questioning if he should, because if Galen wasn't there to see it with him, he wasn't much interested in seeing it either.

He glanced at the Martha's Vineyard shoreline one more time, then got back inside the tank and continued northeast.

The roads, long forgotten by the road crews, were reminiscent of man's first attempt at connecting trading posts. Parts were completely hidden by grass and dirt. Other sections looked like they had never been paved at all. He passed an old football field where the only proof that there had been games played was the single remaining goalpost. The other goalpost and the entire playing field had been taken back by nature. He passed a billboard that had faded completely white under the sun. Whatever message had once been there was now gone and forgotten. He drove over or around fallen trees and other debris.

And finally, after traveling through this apocalyptic stretch of land, headed to Cape Cod. The road offered breathtaking views of water on either side of him. Trees were growing out of the side of miniature cliffs. Others grew out of mounds of rock. The water to the east was rough and choppy, a constant series of waves cutting against the shore. To the west, the water was still. Birds gathered on the latter side because the fish preferred these waters too.

If he had come here with Galen, he would have taken his son to the eastern shore when they wanted to watch the waves, but when it came time to actually get in the water he would have carried his boy to the western shore, where Galen's feet could dangle in the water without fear of an errant wave splashing his face. Everywhere he went it was always what he would have done if Galen were there.

He drove through marshes and forest. There were rocky parts. The sand was a desert bordering every other land type. He even drove past a lake. He could be at the shore, walk on sand to a lake, then walk across more sand to the ocean. Wonders would never cease. Instead of making him glad to have seen it, however, he thought about Galen's charred body and how his boy would never get to see the treasures that the world had to offer.

After all of the beautiful views, man had found a way to ruin the land: at the water's edge was a local airport. It was concrete where only sand belonged, glass instead of brush and marsh. There were times when a man had a revolutionary vision that showed the excellence that people could achieve. It was how airplanes had been made. It was how the Chunnel had been formed. What would Henry IV have thought if you tried to explain the concept of motorized vehicles traveling back and forth, under water, from England to France? The same brilliance made it possible for shuttles to fly out to space and even for the Great De-evolution's food processors.

But then there were times when man's arrogance ruined his capacity for creation. That was how the Mall of America was built. There was no practical reason to build a mall that large. And it was how this godforsaken airport was put in the middle of untainted beach and marsh.

The airport was no LAX or LaGuardia; it was small, the kind found in every Caribbean country, but it was still out of place. It had a single runway, a single hangar, and a few small auxiliary buildings. A prop plane, one tire missing, sat at the corner of a road leading to the runway.

But then the airport did something else than simply irritate him. It made him gasp: a tiny plume of smoke began coming from one of the building's vents.

There were actual people. Living, breathing people.

It was possible they might try to take his tank, but their location was the absolute worst possible choice if their intention was to rob and plunder. Out here in the wilderness, surrounded by water, these weren't people who survived through theft and brutality. But if the fear of violence wasn't keeping him from approaching the airport, what was? After miles and miles of not seeing a new face, of having no one to talk to, he thought he might be happy to run into someone. Instead, he found himself looking behind him, at the path that had brought him here.

A line of people filtered out of the building to stare at his armored machine. Most were smiling. Two were even waving. A little grey-haired man immediately approached as soon as Jeffrey opened the tank's hatch.

"A visitor!" the man said. "Welcome."

He walked right up to the tank, put one hand on it, and with the other arm reached out to shake Jeffrey's hand. The only thing Jeffrey could manage was a simple hello.

In total, there were eight people in the group, all slightly younger than the man shaking Jeffrey's hand, but all older than Jeffrey. A husband and wife, holding hands, stood at the end of the line. Both had completely grey hair and were covered in wrinkles.

The old man asked what brought Jeffrey to them.

"Just always wanted to see what Cape Cod was like," Jeffrey said, feeling dumb as he voiced the words. It was amazing how quickly the ability to be personable vanished when you were alone all the time.

He asked the same of them and one of the women stepped forward to say, "We all just kind of ended up here." She pointed to the married couple before adding, "Only Jeff and Lucy knew each other before we formed into our own little group here."

One of the men asked where Jeffrey was from. A lie seemed easier than the truth. Less painful. He had no idea if the people out here stayed in touch with the outside world.

"Philadelphia," he said, the memory of the place making him look to the southwest to see if smoke clouds were still rising into the air.

One of the women gave a sigh of anguish. One of the men said everything would be OK and patted Jeffrey on his shoulder.

"Have you been keeping up on what's been happening?" one of the other men asked.

"I haven't heard anything. I left after it happened."

"They were turned around when they got to Washington. Nobody there wanted the Philadelphians living with them after what they did. But the caravan had trouble making it back to Pennsylvania. Some of the people refused to attempt the drive back after how long it took to get to Washington, so they found places in the suburbs around D.C. People there say that if you stay up at night you can see folks trying to sneak into Washington to be around other people. They weren't wanted there, but they can't stand being alone, so they try to sneak in and hope people ignore the new faces. Only a quarter of everyone who left Philadelphia ended up making it back safely. Some stayed outside Washington. Some just disappeared. Some simply passed away."

"Are you hungry?" one of them asked when there was silence.

"Would you like to come inside?" another said.

"Are you tired? Have you been traveling long?" yet another asked.

He found himself being led away from the tank and into the airport without being able to consider whether or not it was safe to leave the machine where it was.

Only the old man stayed by Jeffrey's side when they entered the building. They walked by a series of offices that had been converted into bedrooms, with sheets hung across the windows for privacy. They walked by the old office break-room, converted into a real kitchen with two refrigerators, two ovens, and two government-issued food processors. The old man explained that everyone had ended up here after being unhappy with the constant uncertainty of moving south.

"The important thing is to be happy," the man said. "That means different things for different people. For us, it meant peace of mind in knowing where we would be spending each night." As they continued walking, the old man said, "That uncertainty of never knowing where you'll end up drives some people crazy. What's the point of always wanting to go to the next place, always wanting to pack up and head south, if you're always worried while you're doing it? Your final years should be spent enjoying yourself. We didn't work our entire lives just to be slaves to the Great De-evolution."

"So what do you do here?" Jeffrey asked as they passed by the only shower in the entire building.

"Just that. We enjoy ourselves. Some of us go for walks every day. Some of us enjoy reading books or watching movies. We have a pretty good selection of both that we've built up from trips to the nearby towns."

Jeffrey looked around. "I don't mean this to be rude, but it doesn't sound like much."

The wrinkled skin hanging off the old man's throat jiggled when he laughed. "What else do you need?"

Jeffrey didn't have an answer; the old man wouldn't understand what he was talking about if he mentioned Galen's name.

For dinner, everyone sat around a large metal cafeteria table. Some of the bowls scattered around the table had food produced from the food processors, and some contained real fish or vegetables. The last time he ate this much food had been his last meal with Katherine, with Galen sitting beside him. As much as he tried not to let that thought ruin his dinner, he found himself caught up in memories of his boy rather than participating in the conversation going on around him.

When everyone said goodnight and walked to their office/bedroom for the evening, part of Jeffrey thought about sleeping outside in his tank. Instead, one of the women pointed him to a bedroom no one else was using.

He had no idea what he was supposed to do when he woke up the next morning. One of the women was already at the cafeteria table reading a book when he left his room.

She pointed out the window to the beach. "Most of them are already on walks," she said.

He went a mile down the beach without seeing anyone else, then sat down and watched the water and the birds. The old man was waiting for him when Jeffrey got back to the airport.

The two of them walked south along the same road the tank had arrived on. After a while they veered off and walked by some small ponds.

Jeffrey said, "Doesn't it worry you that winter is almost here?"

The old man smiled, which made him appear even more feeble and decrepit. "We'll be fine. We were here last winter and we got by. This winter will be no different."

"What if something happens? What if you have an emergency of some kind and need help?"

The old man seemed confused. "There aren't any hospitals down south either. What does it matter if we are near a hundred people or a thousand people? We have everything we need."

A giant fish came to the surface of one of the ponds before sneaking back underwater again.

"Good water for fishing," the old man said.

But all Jeffrey could think of was how unfair it was that this fish got stuck in a small pond when the entire ocean was on the other side of the sand. Instead of knowing the entire world, it would only ever experience this little pond. It could have gotten lost in the Atlantic, tested the colder waters up north, done anything. Instead, it was trapped, nothing special or distinct about any of it, nothing unique about its life. Somehow, even that made him think of Galen.

"That fish would die if it was in the ocean," the old man said, as if knowing what Jeffrey had been thinking. "It would either get washed ashore by waves or a larger fish would eat it. It has a reason for being exactly where it is."

Jeffrey continued on without saying anything else.

There was nothing he would have changed about the day or about the people or the food. And yet, when everyone went to bed that second night, he waited an hour for everyone to fall asleep before creeping to the front door and pushing it open. He made his way back to the tank and climbed inside.

As soon as the tank's engine was roaring, he started away from the airport, back toward where he had come. When he got about five miles away, far enough that they would no longer be able to hear the engine or find him the next morning, he turned the motor off and went to sleep inside the metal cave. And in the morning, as the sun started to come up, he continued on the path away from the airport.

They were nice people, he told himself, but he wasn't like them. But when he tried to think of what was different between them and himself, he couldn't think of an answer. All he could think about was Galen and the fire and how Katherine could let that happen. He thought about the way the old man spoke of the fish and if he could someday believe that what the old man had been saying was somehow true.

Chapter 12

The skeleton was in the middle of his routine again: "And no one is talking about how many people are going to get sick due to our close proximity to all of the Blocks. Why isn't anyone mentioning that more and more people are getting sick every day? If we take the Blocks with us, we'll all be zombies by the time we get to Washington!"

The next station was at least closer to providing actual news: "Everyone has heard the announcement by now: the city council, along with the Mayor, have agreed that everyone will relocate to Washington one week from today. No additional information on the migration has been provided at this time. Various rallies and protests have already been scheduled for the days leading up to the move."

Instead of calming nerves by announcing a date, Jeffrey knew how people worked—the short timeframe would only add to the general anxiety.

All around the world, people were either going away quietly or were actually celebrating their ends. There were only a handful of countries in the world—Venezuela, Turkey, and Japan—that joined the United States in still having a city they called their capital. Everyone thought New Zealand's government was crazy at first when they announced they would be holding a farewell celebration. The day-long party was a chance for the politicians and their people to have one last holiday before the New Zealand government officially disbanded. It was such a success, a week-long party was held in Buenos Aires when the Argentinian government was ready to close its doors.

In contrast, one day there was a government of Mozambique, and the next day there wasn't. The parliament building was empty and no one ever saw the politicians again. They simply disappeared. The same thing happened in Indonesia, where the people burned down the capital building in frustration at their politicians abandoning them in the middle of the night.

North Korea, of course, was too secretive to let the outside world know what their plans were. As if anyone cared. They would neither confirm nor deny if they were still a government, if they had plans to disband, and if so, if they would celebrate the end. The dictator there was too busy trying to convince everyone else that North Korean scientists had found a cure for the Blocks. No one had believed him the first time he said it, but month after month he kept insisting they would be the only country left after everyone else was extinct. No one paid him any attention.

Jeffrey turned to Katherine. "Promise me you won't take Galen to any of those rallies." When she started to laugh his comment away, he added, "I'm serious. Promise me. I don't want my boy around those people."

"Are we ready for the move?" Katherine asked.

He looked around them. Their dinner plates had been purchased the year before Galen was born, but there would be other plates wherever they went. TVs would be available in any house they went to. They were things that were a part of their lives, but nothing more in the end than a series of objects. They weren't things that needed to be put in the trunk of their car and transported south.

"We're ready," he said. "We don't need any of this."

"I don't want anyone else using our plates when we're gone."

"We aren't burning the house down," he said. She only stared at him. "Don't even think about it. This house and everything in it might be someone else's salvation." She rolled her eyes. "I'm serious," he said. "What if a straggler comes down from New England or Canada and needs a place to live? They would have everything they need here. Let them use our plates. Let them sleep in our beds. Let them live their lives as best they can."

He imagined his grandfather smiling down on him from whatever afterlife he had passed into. It was he who had slapped Jeffrey's wrist when, as a five year-old boy, he had stomped on a large spider.

"That thing had a life," his grandfather had said while Jeffrey rubbed his sore wrist and tried to keep the tears back. "Same as you have a life. Respect that."

These days, when he thought about his grandfather's gruffness that day, he found himself thinking back to all of the other dumb things he had done through his life. The collection of stupidity, of dumb acts built up over the years, made him feel fortunate to still be alive, to have a family at all.

There was the time he had just gotten his learner's permit to drive and thought he was good enough, as a fifteen year-old brat, to drive the family car the way his father did. It only took him five minutes, not even three miles away from the house, to wrap the sedan around a telephone pole.

There was a time in college when his friends got drunk and all took turns jumping from one dorm building to another. They were only two-story buildings, and only eight feet apart, but he should have known better. The first three boys all made the jump successfully, but when Jeffrey took his running start, one of his friends acted like he was going to trip him and Jeffrey stumbled off the edge of the roof and landed in the shrubbery next to the pavement. His supposed friends, all drunk, stared down at the ground in horror. All but one of them ended up running back to their rooms. The final kid was the only one nice enough to call campus security. Jeffrey had a concussion, a broken arm, and a dislocated shoulder. If he had landed one foot to the right, on bare concrete, the doctor thought he might have died.

His life seemed filled with these moments. They hadn't stopped just because the Great De-evolution started or because he became a father. Only three years earlier he had accepted a dare from one of the other men at Fort Dix to call Royal Canadian Air Force bases and tell them that an F-14 had mistakenly been dispatched to firebomb their base and no one could re-establish comms with the plane. Everyone on base should evacuate immediately. Jeffrey only accepted the dare because he thought every base would be abandoned. But on the sixth call, as the men began to lose their interest in the game, a man with a thick French accent answered and Jeffrey gave him the message. The man had probably been at the base by himself after everyone else left for warmer climates. Maybe his family was living on base with him. The sheer panic in his voice made Jeffrey want to confess it was only a joke, but one of the other men hung up the phone before anything else could be said. The poor man had just been minding his own business, hadn't deserved to fear for his life like that. No one did.

After each episode Jeffrey was left realizing how unprepared he was for the realities of life. He was a normal guy, just as likely to crash into a tree as anyone else, just as likely to ruin his liver, just as likely to do something else foolhardy that would leave him breathing out of a tube. He wasn't the rock of stability he wanted to be. Not for himself and not for Katherine. The world was a harsh place. It had been when he was a teenager and when he was a young man, and it still was now. It was only by sheer luck that he was able to get through it all.

Like he knew it would, the mayor's migration announcement spurred a new round of protests and celebrations. Some people were excited. Others resented needing to go in the same caravan as thousands of Blocks. It was difficult, sometimes, to tell which groups were which and if people yelling outside the mayor's office were holding a demonstration or a party.

Katherine said, "I talked to my father today. He sounded worse than usual."

They looked out at their backyard. There was nothing to see except grass and a privacy fence. There were no signs that a child had been raised there. No rusty swing-set. No tire hanging from a tree. No tree house.

"Everything will be all right," he said.

Katherine sighed and put her head against his shoulder. "Every day that goes by is another day he's less capable of making the journey."

He kissed the top of her head. His own parents gave him constant updates on the amount of people funneling down into Florida. California, Texas, and Florida were the only states where the population still remained constant, the daily arrivals from the north off-setting the daily obituaries.

Through it all, Katherine's father's health molded her priorities. Why would she want to take care of a son who had no idea she existed, felt no pain, suffered no loneliness, when she had a father who clearly needed help? What mattered to her, what she knew and saw, was that one person she loved sat quietly without complaining while the other tried to show a brave face but often failed to do so.

After work the next day, instead of going directly home, he drove to his mother and father-in-law's house. Even on his approach, he became alarmed. No one had taken the time to mow their lawn in weeks. The grass came up past his shins.

His mother-in-law ushered Jeffrey inside. She didn't ask why he was showing up unannounced, just closed the front door behind him and said it was nice to see him again. Alan, Katherine's father, was sitting in the living room. An old-fashioned record player offered classical music. The only time Jeffrey thought about classical music was when he visited Katherine's parents. But those times always reminded him how wonderful it was. It made him wish the world could go back to the way it had been when he was a child and there wasn't a single worry in life.

Katherine's father smiled in greeting. Neither of them said anything, however, until the music was done. Jeffrey had no idea who he was listening to, just that he liked it.

"How are you doing these days? How is my daughter doing? How is my grandson?" Alan said after the first piece of music was done and before the next one started.

"Galen is good. The doctor says he's in perfect health."

Katherine's father let his eyes close when he spoke. "Katherine's mother and I were always worried about her when she was growing up. Even when she didn't need us to worry about her. We couldn't help it; she was our daughter. We were her parents. Just like Galen is your son."

Neither of them said anything for a while. The three of them listened to the sounds of piano coming from the turntable. Even more amazing than telescopes that could see far away planets or medical devices that could see torn ligaments was the fact that a pair of human hands could build a piano and then make it produce those noises.

After the next piece came to an end, Alan said, “What brings you here? You’re a nice kid and all, but I never see you here by yourself unless my daughter is upset for one reason or another.”

“We didn’t have an argument.”

The man smiled with his mouth, but not with his eyes. “Let me guess: she’s worried about her mother and me. I’m not surprised. Look at us: we’re old.” He laughed. “That has to be an alarming thing to see—your parents becoming old people. I guess this is a good time to tell you that we won’t be going to Washington with you when the relocation happens.”

Katherine’s mother nodded in agreement.

Jeffrey asked all of the expected questions, but his father-in-law waited until the next piece of music was over before he started up again.

“What are we going to do down in Washington? Live in a place next door to you and Katherine? And when everyone in Washington picks up, are we all going to head down to North Carolina together? Or Florida? What then?” Katherine’s father waved his hands around the room. “This is our home. We have too many memories here. You don’t care about that stuff yet, you’re still young,”—he laughed—“fairly young, so you don’t care about those things. But you will. You’re still too busy living your life to know the importance of the memories you’ve built around yourself. Katherine’s mother and I don’t need to go to Washington. I don’t even like Washington. Too many snotty people.”

"When you get to be our age," Katherine's mother said, "you kind of regain that sense of invincibility you had when you were a kid, except you know how vulnerable you are and you just don't care."

Her husband added: "I grew up listening to my grandfather tell stories about how much the Great Depression affected him. He was never the same afterwards. It haunted him for the rest of his life. He saw people starving in the streets, people throwing themselves out of high-rise windows. By the time World War II started, he wasn't affected by it the way everyone else was. It drove my mother insane because, to her, it was the end of the world. It always infuriated her that my grandparents took it all with a grain of salt. It was the same way for me, being a kid in the 'seventies. All the riots, the protests. Every night there was more footage on the news of the police beating protestors and of body bags being unloaded from giant cargo planes on their way back from Nam. I hadn't lived through the things my grandparents had lived through, so for me, I thought it was the end of the world. My grandfather just smiled at me. I was scared when I was young so that now I can be brave. Brave isn't the right word. I'm not brave, I'm just not afraid. We have everything we need right here."

Jeffrey said, "Katherine will never leave without you."

"She'll have to."

"Help her move on," Katherine's mother said. "Don't let her focus on what's here and what she's leaving behind. Help her focus on what's still to come. That's what's important."

**

He spent the day doing nothing but watching the waves come in and then go back out again. He was staring at the water but he was thinking about Galen's burned corpse rotting in the abandoned city. His boy, his only son, would never be buried or even tossed in a yellow body bag. The charred remains would be rained on, eaten by flies, snowed on, picked apart by crows, until there was nothing left but bone.

After turning the final page of *The Awakening*, he thought it perfectly reasonable to want to walk out into the water and simply disappear into its depths. Each wave beckoned him before retreating back into the ocean. God help him if he read *The Heart is a Lonely Hunter* while he was in a similar mood.

Things wouldn't have been so bad if he could have gone a single day without wondering which part of the stadium Galen was rotting away in. Had he been near where the flames started and died fairly quickly? Or was he in the bleachers, forced to sit there and wait for the flames to spread through the other sections first, enveloping row upon row of Blocks before getting to him? Had Galen died of smoke inhalation before the first flames touched his precious skin, or had he waited patiently in his wheelchair as the fire slowly crept up his legs? Was there anything left of him, or had the bodies all melted together in a twisted collection of blackened limbs? Jeffrey couldn't get the thoughts out of his head.

He tried to imagine his son on the porch with him. The birds would be chirping, the dogs barking somewhere down at the end of the street. He remembered it all as best as he could, but when he imagined Galen there with him, it wasn't his boy that was there, but his burned remains.

And so he said goodbye to the front porch where he spent each night with Galen. He said goodbye to Tyler State Park and even to the Pennsylvania Turnpike.

Occasionally, not often, he wondered what Katherine was doing now. It was doubtful that she would have gone back to their house. Maybe she went to her parents so they could help rationalize what she had done. Knowing her, she would beg and plead with them until they gave up their own plans to stay behind in order to make her happy. Maybe she was living by herself in a house just outside Washington.

None of it mattered. Cleaning pebbles off his pants, he stood up and went back to the tank.

Each day, the roads became less reliable. His progress up the coast, already slow, became even slower. If the tank had to go three miles an hour, that was fine with him.

Sometimes when he was driving he would smell an animal's carcass hidden in the forest and be reminded of what his son's flesh might have smelled like before the flies started picking it apart. Other times, the tank's engine would make a popping noise and he thought of what it must have sounded like as Galen's skin boiled in the inferno.

The tank passed through mile after mile of forgotten highway. Not a single car approached on its way home from a long day at work. No delivery trucks raced away on their final drop-off of the day so they too could get home. It was just him, alone.

He came to a collection of tents set up just off the road. Three of the seven tents had collapsed in a heap on nylon and space-age fabric. The other four were still in good condition. His curiosity got the better of him; against his instincts, he found himself walking toward the little camp. Someone could sneak up from the other direction and take his tank, but the longer he spent driving it the more he realized he wouldn't spend the rest of his life in the armored machine. There would come a time, sooner or later, when he would either abandon it or it would break down and force him to settle wherever it couldn't move anymore.

The ground was mush after all of the snow melted. It only took four steps before his clean shoes were stuck in foot-deep mud. He left them and continued walking with bare feet. Everything below his ankles went numb from the cold slush. But still he walked toward the tents.

"Hello?" he called, but there was no rustling, and no one called out in response. "Is anybody here?"

His answer came in the form of a boot sticking out of one of the fallen tents. Jeffrey pulled the canvas away. An old man in flannel shirts, triple-layered, was lying there, motionless. Dead. The man's skin was unnaturally grayish blue. His eyes were closed in a way that made it possible for Jeffrey to believe the struggling hiker could have had a peaceful death in the middle of sleeping.

Another body was revealed when Jeffrey pulled the tent further away. This one, an old woman, was also frozen. The next tent had two more bodies, and the next after that had one. He unzipped one of the tents that was still standing, proud against the wind. Only one body—maybe the last survivor to succumb to the cold. The next tent was filled with empty food cartons and other trash.

All of the frozen bodies looked like they had simply gone to sleep one night and never woken up again. That was the pretty version of things. More likely, they had struggled to get south, their cars broken down somewhere further up the road, so they tried as best as they could to continue on foot until they reached the next town. Maybe they slept on the side of the road for a week before freezing to death. It could have happened the first night, as soon as the fire went out and no one was awake to restart it. Maybe one of their party had continued on to get help, telling the others he would return with working vehicles. If that had happened, these people might have waited on the side of the road for weeks, hoping in vain that someone was coming to save them, never realizing the other man ran into a pack of wolves, or, perhaps, simply grew too tired and also went to sleep and never woke up.

He didn't offer a prayer. Nor did he look up at the sky and pray that the same thing didn't happen to him. He merely surveyed the scene one last time before walking back, still barefoot, to the tank.

Immediately upon returning to the machine, he wrapped a blanket around his cold feet as tightly as he could. This served two purposes: it warmed his feet quicker, and it kept the tank's interior clean. His feet alternated between searing pain and complete numbness.

When he stopped for dinner that night he found replacement socks and a new pair of shoes. After dinner he came upon a herd of deer in the middle of the road. He counted twenty in all, some with antlers, some without, some fully grown, some young. A few walked off the road as the tank approached, but most remained in the middle of the path without concern. One of the animals even walked closer, as though the tank was interesting instead of the conqueror of battlefields. It was only when the machine was almost nudging them with its turret that the animals stepped off the road and let him pass.

But as soon as the tank started to move forward a little faster, one of the deer darted back out of the woods and ran right in front of his path. Even at the tank's slow speed, Jeffrey didn't have enough time to stop or swerve to the side. The tank, used to running over fallen trees, barely hiccupped as it crushed the deer's ribcage. A wolf darted out of the brush a second later, saw the deer under the tank, and growled in frustration. Without any other options, the wolf disappeared back into the woods.

He popped the hatch and looked at the animal. Somehow, even though half its body was flattened against the road, the deer wasn't dead. Its speed must have gotten it most of the way to safety. Its two back legs, along with its hips and ass were complete mush, stuck against the road like partially cooked batter. The front half of the deer, still in shock, continued the struggle to get away. It was glued, though, unable to drag the back half of its body off the road.

It screamed and screamed.

"Oh Jesus," Jeffrey said, his hands reaching out as though to sooth the deer.

But when he lowered himself to the ground, the animal, in addition to its nauseating screams, it began to buck with its front legs. As much as it tried to run away from the road, as much as it thrashed with its two good hooves, it couldn't go anywhere. The screams went on without pause. In front of him was an animal completely crazed by oncoming death. There was nothing it could do to save itself and that only served to make it even more scared.

"Jesus, please stop," Jeffrey said. "Please stop."

The deer kept thrashing against the ground. It kept crying. Jeffrey spun in a circle, looking for something, anything, to make the situation better. The only things around him were the woods and the tank.

"I'm so sorry," he said before dropping back into the tank. And then, lining the machine up again, he drove it forward once more. The deer's screams ended the instant the tank began to run over it a second time.

It would take him a long time to look back and realize he wasn't upset that the animal was dead—his parents would have both done the same thing in his place—it was that, right in front of his eyes, a living thing had lost everything it had known. Something had changed into nothing. The other deer in its group would never see it again. It would never give birth to more fawns. It would never settle down for the night and provide warmth to the rest of the huddled animals. Life had given way to the absence of life. With the appearance of the Blocks, it was impossible not to be familiar with the concept, but he didn't like seeing it right in front of him. He didn't like being a part of it.

The tank continued north.

Chapter 13

A segment on one of the news shows that night devoted ten minutes to a woman who claimed she could see ghosts. But not regular ghosts. She claimed to be able to see, exclusively, the ghosts of dead Blocks. The segment's host started by insinuating it was convenient that the woman claimed only to see the ghosts of people who couldn't talk back and provide relatives with proof they were really there, but after giving the audience a skeptic's minute, the rest of the show seemed to take her quite seriously.

"Tell us about these ghosts," the segment's lead said. "What are they like?"

Instead of wearing a somber black outfit, as one might expect of a woman tormented by spirits, the fortune-teller turned ghost-seer wore a sparkling blue blouse that was accentuated by layer upon layer of makeup.

"The first thing I'd like everyone to know," she said, grimacing, "is that this isn't some fairytale ability that I'm lucky to have. I don't want this miraculous ability. It's something I'm forced to live with."

"But why wouldn't you want to be able to see the ghosts?" The interviewer was a recent addition to the show. Without universities offering degrees in Communications anymore, he had no background or skill-set suitable for making him on-air talent except he was unbelievably handsome. This inexperience led him to take people at face value and get caught up in his own questions; he really wanted to know why someone wouldn't want to be able to see ghosts!

The woman offered another pained smile. “Because they don’t do anything. These aren’t normal ghosts we’re talking about. These ghosts don’t talk. They can’t tell you what they want. They can’t communicate with you, can’t tell you what’s keeping their soul trapped in this plane. They can’t even point at the picture of someone who killed them so the killer is brought to justice. They just sit there and stare at you.” When the interviewer didn’t immediately respond, she added, “It’s really creepy.”

“It sounds awful. Tell us, why do you think you were picked to have this ability?”

“I’m not sure. I’ve always had a special power in one way or another. In high school, I had visions of the future. In—“

“Did you foresee the Great De-evolution?”

“No, nothing like that. I knew exactly which day Bobby Brinkle was going to ask out my best friend, though.”

“That’s great.” But you could tell from the way the young interviewer slumped back in his chair that he was disappointed that an already great story hadn’t turned into what would have been an Emmy winning story, had the Emmy’s still been around.

“Anyway, after high school, I could tell people’s fortunes. That ability went away after a while, but then I started to be able to see peoples’ past lives. And now, I can see ghosts. But only Block ghosts.”

“Describe to us exactly what it’s like.”

“It’s ghastly! You want to be able to help them. I know they need help or else they wouldn’t be haunting me, but I have no idea what they want. They just keep staring straight ahead. When I notice them, they're always staring straight at me. But if I get up to go to the kitchen, they just keep staring at the wall until they disappear. The poor things can't even follow me with their eyes."

"And do they appear like normal people?"

"That's the thing. They appear the way they were at the moment they died. And Blocks are still too young to die from natural causes. If you're seeing a Block ghost, you're seeing it because it died in a pretty unpleasant way. The bodies I see have been tortured by sickos, or have been picked apart by animals after they were abandoned on the side of the road. Normally, these ghosts would want some sort of acceptance with what happened."

"Did a ghost tell you that?"

"No, no, that's just what I've always seen on TV and in the movies. But these poor kids can't tell me who killed them or what would give them peace. They're doomed to spend the rest of eternity as motionless ghosts unless I can figure out a way to communicate with them. No one should have to suffer their fate. It's bad enough they were abused in some pervert's basement or thrown away like trash, they don't deserve to spend eternity in some kind of Block purgatory. No one deserves that."

The screen went black.

"I refuse to watch this bullshit for even one more minute," Jeffrey said as he left the room to go check on Galen. But he knew, even after he had left, that Katherine would be scared to sleep in the dark, lest a Block ghost visit them and gaze at her as she tried not to have too many nightmares.

**

Growing up, the Boston skyline was always shown before and after commercial breaks for Celtics games. But from where Jeffrey scanned the view, from Highway 3, the shining city he remembered seeing as a boy was replaced by a horizon of broken buildings, a ghost town of old corporations.

A deserted diner still had most of the ingredients to make pancakes. There was no fresh milk but a food processor took care of that part. He also had the machine make him chocolate chips since the one bottle of chocolate syrup he found had mold growing all over it.

The diner's radio still functioned, but only one station offered music. Beethoven or Bach, a piece he had once heard at Katherine's parents' house, echoed throughout the diner. Every other station was gone.

The diner was covered with framed 8x10 glossy pictures of celebrities and athletes who had stopped by to taste the world famous burgers and milk shakes. Most everyone in the photos had long since passed away. The few young celebrities, now senior citizens, had disappeared to warmer parts of the world. Had he any intention of staying in the diner for longer than one meal, he would have removed all of these pictures from the walls; there was no need to be reminded of the once-smiling people who were all gone.

An old newspaper was still sitting on top of the counter. In big letters across the page he read, *Beantown Welcomes Quebec, Eh?* The story went on to talk about how the Canadian city was readying to evacuate and join with the people in Boston. Montreal and Ottawa were expected, the paper said, to make similar decisions in the next year. This was, of course, long before Boston itself was the focus of rumors centering around exactly when they would head south to New York City. The Boston newspapers had all shut down by that time.

The city hadn't stood a chance after the Red Sox and Celtics both disbanded during the same year. Maybe if only one of the teams had quit and fans could still go to Fenway or the Garden to see the other, morale wouldn't have plummeted so quickly. Seeing both teams play their last game within months of each other, the city had nothing to root for, nothing to cheer. If ever the importance of sports to a city was questioned, it was reiterated during those months of the Great De-evolution. People started leaving for New York without waiting for the official migration. Senior citizens seemed to be dying quicker than in the states where the Lakers still played the Spurs or the Braves still played the Astros.

With his belly full, Jeffrey continued north into the city center. He thought about going in a loop around the city because of the horror stories of frozen bodies scattered around each city block and the rumors that there were still tiny tribes fighting for survival, all stark raving mad from the suffering and isolation. Nobody ever went north to see if these people really existed, but the rumors continued because they thrived without needing any proof. Like Bigfoot and the Loch Ness monster, someone had spoken to someone else who had supposedly been near the city and heard terrible cries or seen recent footprints in the snow. That was enough to keep the rumors going.

He let the tank veer off the highway, toward signs pointing to abandoned universities. In the old days, each year's graduating class would fill these streets after a night of revelry and drinking. Now, the streets were empty except for stray cats everywhere. There were cats sitting under the trees, looking up at the mocking birds singing their songs, and there were cats sleeping next to the sewers, ready to slip away at the smallest threat. Cats were walking up and down the sidewalks, mimicking the actions of the former ruling class. Cats were jumping in and out of broken storefront windows, some coming out with rats or mice in their mouths; others, not as lucky, coming out with their mouths empty. They were everywhere he looked.

At City Hall, a statue of Lady Justice was still holding the scales of justice in one hand, but her other hand, along with the sword it was supposed to be holding, had cracked and broken. Chunks of rock lay on the ground in pieces. He saw the famous *Cheers* bar, where no one would be drinking beer anymore. It might be full of bodies, however. Better to remember the laughs on TV and not see what the reality had become.

The entire city looked like London—if the city had never been rebuilt after World War II. Some of the skyscrapers had broken open, leaving piles of rubble on the ground. Nearly all of the windows were missing from the corporate offices. A bank had collapsed in on itself. In ten years Philadelphia would look the same way. In fifteen years, Washington would look this way. In twenty-five years, Atlanta would be identical. In forty years, only a few years after the last men and women had taken their final breaths in the great Florida sun, Miami would look this way. Did all of the people heading south think they were outrunning death, or did they know there was only so far they could travel before they ran into southern waters? And Death, taking her good ol' time traveling down 95, would eventually catch up with them. When they were dispatched, she would load her scythe into a boat and cross the water to Cuba, then the rest of the Caribbean.

It wasn't until he was heading back toward the highway that he saw the first man.

There was a disconnect between what he expected to see and what his eyes revealed to him. The man in front of him wasn't crazed, bearded, and wide-eyed, a sawed-off shotgun slung over his shoulder. He was merely a man of ninety, struggling, even with the assistance of a cane, to walk. Jeffrey stopped the tank and opened the hatch.

"Hello there," he said, smiling at this old man who was almost slipping and falling with every step he took toward the tank.

The man grumbled words that Jeffrey couldn't understand. Each step brought the pitiful man minutely closer to the tank. Something in the man's broken down face kept Jeffrey from offering assistance. It might have been how he never took his eyes off the machine. Even when he stumbled, almost fell, he stared, as though in a trance, at the metal monster. The hobbling man was the closest thing to a zombie that the Great De-evolution could produce. A truck could come hurtling down the street and the man would pay it no attention, even as it ran him over, because he was mindlessly staggering towards this armored machine in front of him.

"How are you doing?" Jeffrey said. And then, when that didn't get a response, "Can I help you? Do you need help?"

The decrepit man continued forward without trying to answer. Then another man appeared. This one wasn't quite as old, maybe only seventy-five or eighty. The newcomer quickly passed the man struggling with his cane.

Jeffrey smiled at this new man walking toward him. "How are you doing? Nice day out."

But this man also walked toward the tank without responding. And when he got to the tank, instead of reaching up to shake Jeffrey's hand, he simply tried to climb up the tread.

"What are you doing?" Jeffrey said, still not understanding what was going on. "You're going to hurt yourself."

The man started to pull himself up in an attempt to stand on top of the tank's tread. His grip wasn't strong enough, though. Right as he tried to lift his first foot up, his fingers slipped away and he fell backwards with a loud grunt.

"Sir, are you all right?"

The man got back to his hands and knees. The original man was still twenty feet away, making a shameful amount of progress toward the tank. He was gasping for air so heavily that it was doubtful he would ever make it to where Jeffrey was. But the second man was now successfully pulling himself up onto the tank, and once there, was trying to push Jeffrey aside in order to descend into the machine's core.

"What are you doing?" Jeffrey said, but would never get a response.

He pushed back at the man just enough to stop his progress. This seemed to puzzle the grizzled, old man, who was still singularly focused on getting inside the tank.

Finally Jeffrey could understand what the other man was mumbling: "Take me with you. Please, take me with you. Need to leave. Please."

Two more people, both exceedingly ancient, appeared at the same intersection. They too began making their way toward the tank. The old man standing next to Jeffrey put a hand over Jeffrey's mouth in an attempt to push him away. Jeffrey pushed back. The man lost his footing and fell off the side of the vehicle before disappearing out of view. But by this time, two of the other men, both walking with the assistance of canes, were at the tank as well.

All three men were clambering up now. Six hands strained to pull their owners closer to the tank's hatch. Each man begged Jeffrey to save them.

None of them were listening, none of them even realized Jeffrey was heading north instead of toward the remains of civilization. He pulled the hatch shut, then motored the tank toward the other side of the street. One of the men immediately fell off the tank and remained motionless on the ground. Another of the old men hung on to the back of the tank for twenty feet as it dragged him across the intersection before he too finally let go.

A third man tried to jump on the tank as it passed. Maybe, as a spry young man he could have made the leap, but in his old age, hobbling just to get close to the tank, he managed only a slight stumble forward. The tank ran over his foot, crushing every bone in it. The man howled in pain.

Jeffrey drove the tank three blocks away, enough distance to be sure he was out of their elderly range. At a city park, he stopped and popped the hatch again. There was no trace of the crazed senior citizens. One of them was probably crying, another was likely still begging for Jeffrey to take him away. None of them could be heard, though.

The park he stopped at wasn't unlike parks where he and Katherine and Galen had gone back home. Couples had likely come here, back before the end was signaled, had laughed together, their dogs chasing Frisbees. The harbor would be full of boats coming and going. All of that was gone now.

Another man appeared. This man was slightly younger than the others, wasn't walking with a limp yet.

His hand dangled by his side, a pistol held gingerly, no intent to use it. The sight of it made Jeffrey reseal the tank's hatch, but on his way inside he thought he saw the man wave his arms as if to mock Jeffrey's panic.

From inside the tank, Jeffrey yelled out, "Don't shoot, I won't hurt you."

"That's good to know, friend. I'm no match for a tank."

But when Jeffrey peeked back out again, the man was still approaching, still carrying the gun.

"Don't come any closer," Jeffrey warned.

The man chuckled. "Why not? I only want to talk."

"You have a gun."

"My friend, you have a tank."

"Put the gun down and we can talk."

"Put the tank down and we can talk."

When Jeffrey looked over the top of the hatch, he saw the other man had put the gun down on a wooden bench before starting toward him again. The man stopped ten feet from the tank. Without the threat of bullets, Jeffrey pulled himself out of the machine and lowered himself to the ground.

"What are you all doing here?" Jeffrey asked, even though it was this man who had sought him out.

"Someone had to stick around and see our fair city off." The man looked around for effect. "The park is deserted. As is the harbor. Sadly, even the bars." This last part made the old man give a pained smile, made him wipe away an invisible tear. "The name is Garth. Nice to meet you."

"What about everyone back there, Garth?" Jeffrey said, motioning to the other side of the highway. "Are any of them seriously hurt?"

"We have all been seriously hurt, my friend," the other man said. "At one time or another."

"But are they hurt, now?"

"I won't lie: probably they are. Even a minor injury is serious these days. We are old, and there are no doctors. A broken bone won't get set. A cut will get infected. You know how it goes. But that's life. C'est la vie. It's not a sad thing, it's just part of life. Speaking of which, what brings you here, my friend? You still haven't introduced yourself."

"I was just traveling through. Jeffrey. My name is Jeffrey."

He took his eyes off Garth just long enough to make sure no one else was sneaking up from the other direction. This caused the man to smile.

Garth rubbed the edge of his grey beard with his palm, then motioned to the other side of the highway. "Those were actually the healthier ones over there. Don't worry, no one is going to hijack your ride." And then, when Jeffrey didn't say anything, he added, "Are you really going to make me ask the question?"

"Why am I driving a tank?"

The man laughed. "No, friend. Why are you heading north instead of south?"

"I don't know. I guess I just didn't want to go the same direction as everyone else."

"Why are you driving a tank?"

"It gets me where I need to go."

Garth laughed with childish delight.

Jeffrey asked why he had a gun.

"For my own sanity, my friend. No other reason. None of the other people here have their wits about them enough to cause me harm. That little piece of metal," the man said, pointing to the tiny pistol on the bench, "makes me feel safe, much the same way I imagine your big piece of metal"—he motioned to the tank—"makes you feel safe."

"You could have shot me when I had my head out."

"My friend, if I was that good of a shot I would have done more exciting things in my life than attend board meetings and run marathons back when those things were still in vogue. How about you? What did you do in your life?"

"I was in the military."

This made Garth laugh again. "You arrived in a tank. Of course you were in the military. But what did you do with your life?"

Jeffrey didn't know how to answer this. He kept expecting to see the senior citizens hobbling across the street, begging for a ride out of the city. None of them appeared, however.

"So what are you doing next?" Garth said.

"I guess I'll just keep going north."

"Until you run out of land?"

"Something like that. How about yourself? What will you do next?"

"My friend, there is no next for us." He motioned around at the once great city, known for its history, its personality, its pride—now void of all of those things, only barren and quiet. "We stayed here when the others left because this was our home. Some of us were probably scared of change. Some of us were too proud to leave the old life we held dear."

"And how about you? Why do you still stay?"

The man smiled. He seemed a little more tired each time he gave his fake smile. "My friend, I could say it was because I hate New York, but it's not. I could say it's because I like the winters here, but it's definitely not that either. I just didn't want to spend the rest of my life picking up and heading south each time a city started to empty out too much. I was happy here, so I figured I might as well stay."

Jeffrey expected the man to ask again why he was traveling north, but he didn't. Instead, Garth said, "Do you know why everyone is heading south?"

"To be around other people."

The man gave a wave of the hand. "Incorrect, my friend."

"To be where it's warm?"

The man did his impression of a buzzer going off. "That is also incorrect. They aren't heading south because they need the comfort of being surrounded by others. And they aren't afraid of some snow. They are heading south because they are trying to keep things how they used to be. Not the house, not even the city, has to be the same. Those things can change quite easily. What they are trying to keep consistent is the sense of how things were before all of this started. They want to feel like things are still normal for as long as they can. That's what being around other people, seeing neighborhoods full of happy families, gives them. The sooner they can come to terms with the Great De-evolution, to understand it is out of their power, that they can only have the lives they have today, not the lives they had yesterday, that is when they will be OK with where they are. When they understand that, they probably won't be so eager to make the next move south."

Jeffrey didn't think that was true. Everyone he saw in Philadelphia, Katherine included, really had wanted to be around as many other people as possible. After the blizzard that wiped out Boston, everyone really had wanted to be where it was warm.

Garth saw the look of skepticism on his face, saw the next question that was going to form and answered it before Jeffrey needed to speak. "If that were true, my friend," he said, "then why are they burning their houses down before they leave? Why are they concerned with being surrounded by Blocks? It's because they are afraid to have a new set of memories, but the old ones are also too painful to keep holding onto. Going south, trying to outrun the inevitable, lets them ignore how stuck they are. But when you can appreciate the old memories, while also creating new ones, then you are truly a rich man. Richer than if you could turn lead into gold, that's for sure."

"What about the people back there," Jeffrey asked. "They're still begging to get south."

The man nodded. "Sadly, they haven't come to accept this conclusion yet. When they do, if they ever do, they will likely realize getting south doesn't give them anything that being here can't provide."

"Why don't you explain it to them?"

"My friend, there are some things you have to learn for yourself. I have surely told each of those people back there what I've told you, but it's up to them to accept it. They may never get to that point, but the nice thing is it only takes one day for it to happen, and each new day is a new chance for it to occur."

Neither of them said anything as Jeffrey considered what had been said.

"Be safe," Garth said finally, beginning to stand. "And on your way out of here, make sure you take the expressway or 93. Don't bother taking the tunnels. Someone blew them up a couple of years ago." And then he smiled once more, but a genuine smile this time.

It crossed Jeffrey's mind that he should shake Garth's hand, but he was already walking back to the bench where the gun was. With it in hand, he turned and waved goodbye, then disappeared around the corner to where the pile of broken men were probably still on the ground, each with fractured hips or backs.

The tank rumbled up Highway 1 because it kept Jeffrey close to the water. And when presented with the opportunity, he veered off the highway and took the local road running along the coast so he could see the waves and the sand. After being in the city, he needed to see the beach again. And as the sight and sound of the waves calmed him, he thought about all the things the man had said and if there could be any truth to it.

Chapter 14

Back when he enlisted in the army, he never thought there would be a day when he and the other few remaining officers would celebrate being the last men on base. Appropriately, the cake they were eating had sugary icing designed to look like an American flag draped across an empty battlefield. There were two trenches, some artillery, but no men on either side to continue fighting the war.

They also had donuts and cookies. Some of these had frosting to make them resemble grenades with the pins still in place. There was also beer. But the men didn't call it beer, they called it *End of the Military Brew*. Halfway through the party a cork popped—a final gunshot—and champagne sprayed out.

The men were all laughing and clapping and hugging. Jeffrey seemed to be the only one who didn't understand why they were cheering. They might as well be celebrating the end of the Super Bowl or the final Christmas. The men retold stories they had all told a hundred times before. They toasted to everything they could think of. Meanwhile, Jeffrey stood by the corner and watched them.

Yes, the boxes of paper were tedious. Yes, the routines and bureaucracy were smothering. But there was also history and tradition, and that meant a lot. He was perfectly fine with not having another annual performance review or printing off another series of monthly audits littered with arrow-shaped flags where his superiors had to provide their signature. But this going away party was a celebration that proved all the paperwork they filed was nothing more than a wasted forest. Wasted time. It was a party to announce that their weekly staff meetings were simply time away from their friends and families, nothing more.

Unlike the parties they had for promotions, no family members were around to take part in the festivities. The men with regular children would have felt bad bringing their sons and daughters to a party where the other men had their Block children sitting motionless in chairs around the table. It was for the better. He wouldn't have to act like he hadn't overheard such things as: "I hope they don't make me sick," or "Look at it. It can't do anything for itself," or "We're going to have thousands of them to take with us to Washington," or "My parents never used to be sick. Now they're sick all the time."

An ancient white-haired man, who no one recognized, sat at the conference room table and told everyone what it had been like to serve in the military forty years earlier, back when most of the men in the room were still pissing themselves. No one knew how he had heard about their celebration, but they toasted him all the same.

As much as the men tried to focus on the celebration at hand, some of them couldn't help but talk about the upcoming migration south. These were the same men who couldn't keep themselves from talking about work during holiday parties. One of them said it sounded like another rally was taking place near the stadium, but the rest of the room didn't pay attention.

After an hour, Jeffrey couldn't take any more and went back to his office. He closed the door so the noise coming down the hallway was blotted out. The only things he could think about were Galen's body being dropped next to the telephone pole as if he was nothing more than an empty box or unwanted trash, his next-door neighbor's burning house, and the drunken man's threats toward the helpless dog. What chance did his boy have in a world where people did these things? What hope was there for him or for anyone else? The more he thought about the uncertainties of a declining population, the more he gave credence to Katherine's constant worrying. He shouldn't be so dismissive toward her.

His fingertips were covered with a layer of thick dust from where they had been touching his desk. He was here every day, yet his office looked like it thought he had been gone for ten years already. It was amazing how quickly the world could wipe something away. Already, there were reports that Great Falls looked like it had been abandoned since the gold rush, void of people, covered in a blanket of dirt, collapsed buildings. It was simply what happened once the city was vacated and nature returned. Parts were flooded while other parts resembled Death Valley.

He wished he could be the type of person who didn't notice the dust on boxes, or could at least ignore it. The men down the hall in the conference room, laughing and partying as if there wasn't a single worry in the world, were all able to ignore the dust. There were other fathers down the hall with Block children who were Galen's age. They were eating vanilla cake with colorful icing while Jeffrey was alone in his office.

**

Every day he ran across a new place he had never heard of before, places like Swampscott and Marblehead. And every day he found places he had heard of but never been to, places like Salem and Gloucester. At each place, he stopped and looked for gas stations, grocery stores, and a library. The museums in Salem had been, ironically enough, burned to the ground years earlier. Sometimes he stayed in a town for a night or two, and sometimes he stayed for a month or an entire season. He kept track of time only by the color of the leaves and by the eventual appearance and disappearance of snow.

He went through a phase where he only read books that focused on history's great leaders, reading varying accounts of the lives of Alexander the Great, Genghis Khan, and Napoleon, before following those up with books about Roosevelt, Rabin, and Churchill. Book after book, he read about conquered lands, ends of dynasties, and men leading other men to achieve more than they thought themselves capable of. He noticed a theme of great leaders almost always suffering great loss.

At Ipswich, not even the tank would be able to pass through the line of fallen trees and sunken roads ahead of him, and he had to go northwest just long enough to get to 95 for a while. At Expressway 101 he could have gone west to see one of the many state parks or continued past them into the vastness of endless lands. At Highway 16 he had a chance to see the giant Lake Winnipesaukee and the White Mountain National Forest, but he stayed near the coast then too.

At Kennebunkport, he spent a day trying to find the place where the world's leaders had once stayed. There was no sign that they had ever been there. Most of the buildings and homes were so dilapidated that there would soon be no sign that anyone had been there at all, let alone presidents and prime ministers.

Slowly, he began to forget these were all places where people had once lived. It happened for the first time in Portland. He had a quick thought that it was odd to be the only person to see this city before remembering thousands of other people had once called it their home. It began to seem normal that no one had ever been around these parts. By the time he got to Freeport, he spent the walk from the coffee shop to the library trying to imagine what it might have been like to have other people on the sidewalks, cars driving past, phones ringing. Later, it even became difficult to imagine Galen with him in these cities. They were completely new places in the history of his life, completely separate from anything he had previously known.

He stayed in Bangor for half a year, but being away from the water kept the thought in his mind that he should start moving again eventually. A few times a week he emailed his parents a little story of something he had seen during his travels. He never mentioned Katherine. Only occasionally did he mention Galen. The responses he got back always said something about how happy his mother and father were that he was seeing the world, even if it was the Great De-evolution's version of the world he was touring. He knew what they meant: cafés with no one at the other tables, docks with no sailboats. They never asked when he was coming down to Florida. They never made him feel guilty for going away from the equator when everyone else raced toward it.

It was only when a group of four hikers, two men and two women, saw the smoke coming from his chimney, that he finally started thinking about moving on again.

Both couples were married to their high school sweethearts, and each of them had been lifelong friends. They were from a town just north of Quebec.

"We were the final ones," one of the men said. "The winters weren't any worse, but every year they *seemed* a little worse, you know." The other three shook their heads in agreement. "So we finally decided to set off. We made it about twenty miles before our van wasn't worth driving anymore. Since then, we've been walking. Some days we walk ten miles. Other days we only walk one. And some days we don't go anywhere, you know."

One of the women told Jeffrey he was the first person they had seen since their town emptied out to join Quebec. By the time they set off on foot, every other town had been deserted as well.

"There are some people living out on Cape Cod," Jeffrey offered. As soon as he mentioned it, though, he wished he'd kept his mouth shut; there was no way these people would make it that far, and it wasn't fair to get their hopes up when they had been happy making as much or as little progress as they saw fit.

When they asked where he was from, he pointed south. One of the women asked how much longer Jeffrey thought he was going to be living there.

He didn't have a better answer than, "I'm really not sure. I guess when I finally get tired of this place, I'll move on." But he already knew, seeing the campers, that he would be gone soon.

The five of them stood in the middle of I-95, where cars had once faced fog and rush-hour traffic to get to work.

They shared a meal together, courtesy of Jeffrey's food processor. While they ate, he didn't say anything about himself, and because he didn't, they didn't offer more about themselves.

When he woke up the next morning, he saw smoke coming out of the chimney three houses down the street from him. The Canadians didn't come back over that morning, or even at regular intervals, but they were constantly around. He went for fewer walks because when he did he inevitably ran into one of them. He went to the library less because they interrupted his reading. He heard one of the couples laughing as they passed by his house on a walk. When there was a knock on his front door while he was reading about the Dust Bowl, he thought about ignoring it. One of the women had come down to see if he would like to have dinner with them that evening. He lied and said he didn't feel well.

He just wanted quiet. They were nice people, there was absolutely nothing wrong with them, but he just wanted quiet.

One day, one of the Canadians knocked on his door and asked if he would like to sit and chat for a while. But as soon as the Canadian hiker started talking, it was about things Jeffrey didn't want to hear.

"You know, when the Great De-evolution first started, there was a popular reality TV show up in Canada called *Growing Up Block*. You ever heard of it?"

Jeffrey said he hadn't.

"It focused on this couple that tried to have as many Blocks as possible. They found some doctor dumb enough to give them fertility treatments and the woman ended up having seven Blocks at once. What is that called, septuplets? And that was in addition to the two other Blocks she'd already given birth to. Anyway, this camera crew followed the couple and their Blocks all around Quebec. The producers even bought them a bigger home to make it easier for them to film the family. At the end of the first season, the finale revealed she was pregnant once again. With twins this time."

Jeffrey groaned. "Christ, what's wrong with

people?"

"I know, but it gets worse. By the end of the second season the ratings were bad and the city was talking about relocating south, so they tried to think of what would make for the best TV. They could follow the family as they went south, but they didn't like that idea. The parents were the ones that came up with the idea to take all of their Block kids to Niagara Falls. One-by-one, they sent each kid over the falls in a barrel. The kids who survived would go to Boston, the ones who didn't, wouldn't. In all the time they planned the finale, neither of the parents and no one involved with the show asked if there was something seriously wrong with what was going to happen. They just cared about their ratings and their fame. Five of the eleven kids survived the falls. But news got out about what happened before the show even aired and everyone involved was arrested. Except the parents. They vanished. Some people said they were murdered and buried. Other people reported having seen them in Miami where no one would know them."

"Why are you telling me this? I don't like hearing about this sort of thing."

"I don't know," the Canadian hiker said. "When I heard what happened in Philadelphia, it made me think about that couple and what they did to their Blocks, and how everyone else around them just got caught up in it. I guess it's human nature."

"If it's human nature, I'm glad I'm here instead of wherever they are."

The Canadian only nodded in agreement.

Jeffrey found himself grumbling under his breath the rest of the day. Was that the man's way of apologizing for what had happened amongst his northern neighbors, or was it the man distancing himself from it? Why even bring it up in the first place? And why say it was human nature? It wasn't. Why was it so hard for people to remember what life had been like before the Great De-evolution began? There had been murder and rape and pain and suffering, but they hadn't been the norm. And they hadn't been apologized for, hadn't been explained away as human nature. It was a travesty to say it had become part of our nature just because our final days were in sight. The Greeks and Romans, the French and British, everyone in between, hadn't brought us to this point just to think there were understandable circumstances when you could ignore your friends and family, when you could let them sit in flames until their eyelids melted shut, or let them go into the Falls until their lungs were full of water. We were supposed to be better than that.

After all their traveling, the Canadians were just happy to be around another person. It didn't matter that Jeffrey had a tank parked in the middle of 95, that he didn't tell them anything about himself, or that he stayed in his house more than he spoke to them. They just liked knowing that another human was nearby.

As he sat in his new, inherited house, he looked around at the books and clothes scattered around the floor. It was amazing how quickly possessions built up, even on this trip. He had started with nothing more than the clothes he was wearing. Now, he had two backpacks full of items he didn't think he could live without. He had four pairs of pants, three shirts, two sweaters, and a collection of socks and underwear. Books filled each corner of the room. Waiting back at the tank for him were his map, another pair of shoes, and some heavy winter clothes.

Once everything was loaded into the tank, he verified distances on his map, then started the engine. The Canadians' house was far enough away from the highway that he would be gone before they could run out on the street and wave him down.

The two couples would wake up the next day by themselves. He didn't think they would much care one way or the other. Just by the way they smiled when hearing bad news and good news alike, he could tell they had long ago learned that ups and downs were part of life. They were smart enough to realize they had settled into a nice town, a place worth living in if Jeffrey was there or if he was gone. Maybe they would attempt the walk all the way down to Cape Cod. If that was the goal they set for themselves, he hoped they achieved it.

Chapter 15

Men were still gathered in the conference room. There was silence now, however, as they all watched TV and ignored the cake and beer. A rally near the stadium had turned into a chance for the migration's planners to store as many of the Blocks as they could gather in one place, to "get them ready for the trip south" as one person on TV had put it, by getting them organized at the stadium two days prior to when the busses would leave the city.

To Jeffrey, it was madness that someone could drop off their brother or sister or son or daughter at the feet of strangers. Maybe these people tried to convince themselves that their Block would get better care this way. What Jeffrey knew was that none of those people, back when society offered a semblance of normality, would have given something as trivial as their wallet to a stranger if the request had been made. So why would they now be willing to put the health and safety of their loved ones in the hands of people who made jokes about Blocks, degraded them? Some of the same people who now offered to load Blocks into the stadium had recently been holding cardboard signs reading things like, "Why should I have to worry about your Block?" and "No voice, no spot in my caravan." They put these signs down to help load bodies into the stadium.

And the Blocks' families let them. It would have seemed crazy if a man walked up to you and said, "Can I have your social security number?" or "Let me store your driver's license in my wallet for safe keeping." But a Block, a person who couldn't watch out for their own self-interest, was given up as though a stadium was just as good as their own bed.

Surely, Katherine couldn't be one of the people who would think that might be a good idea.

He dialed her cell phone to make sure she was at home, but it rang and rang without her answering. If she would have just answered, just been at home, he would have been able to go back to watching the scene play out on the television. When her recorded voice told him to leave a message, he imagined one of these random men, who didn't even like Blocks, ushering Galen to a seat near the field, surrounded on all sides by other Blocks.

Had she been out running errands anyway, or had she seen the calls to bring your Block downtown and thought it a reasonable thing to do? As he walked toward his car, her phone went to the answering machine again.

If he could just hear his wife's voice, be reassured that his boy was alive, everything would be better. It wouldn't matter that the population was dying or that people seemed to have forgotten what was important in the world; holding his boy in his arms would make up for all of that.

His fingers rustled through his pocket as he ran, causing his car keys to fall out. Not wanting to stop running as he picked them up, he accidentally punted the keychain across the parking lot. A string of curses exploded from his mouth. His shoulder bumped into a Mercedes so hard that the side mirror tore off. Frustrated, he kicked it too. His keys were under the tire of an abandoned Porsche. He grabbed them and dashed back to his car.

As he raced off the base, he could already see, up ahead, that traffic was slowing. His car horn blared. He yelled. He banged on his steering wheel until he saw why the other drivers were slowing and staring: a small stream of smoke had begun to rise from the stadium. The man on the radio sounded alarmed.

Please, God, no.

**

In giant letters, a billboard told him, "Leaving the United States. Canada welcomes you." Behind it, another billboard had fallen over, its message forgotten in mud. An immigration guard shack was covered with bird shit, all of its windows missing. The practice of checking passports into and out of the country hadn't existed for over a decade. For all intents and purposes, the invisible border between the two countries wasn't even imaginary anymore—it wasn't there at all.

Just off the road, only a few steps from the guard shack, a rope was swaying back and forth in the breeze, a noose at its end. Below it, bones were scattered on the ground. The body must have been hanging from the rope until the flesh rotted away and the bones fell. A white ribcage was intact, but a piece of faded brown cardboard was still tied around it, as it must have been back when the body had flesh. Any message that had once been written there, either of vengeance or threat, had long ago faded away in the sun.

It wasn't long before he came to the end of I-95 and had the option of going north on Canadian Highway 2 or taking it slightly south and then east. Already, the leaves were orange and red and falling off the trees. At the first sign of snowflakes, he pulled the tank into an abandoned neighborhood and used another house as his temporary home.

The snowstorms were bad. For a week straight he couldn't open the front door to his house because drifts of snow blocked him in. The tank, protected under a tarp, contributed to a snow bank two stories tall. Without plows to clear a path for him, it would be months before he could think about continuing on the roads again.

It seemed like it was almost summer by the time all the snow cleared. He drove for hours without seeing a single house. At the end of the first night he slept on top of his tank, next to the swollen banks of a river he didn't see on his map. After all the snow, he was surprised there wasn't more flooding. He wondered what happened to the rest of the world in places where no one was around to control the water level at dams. Entire cities would vanish under water. Was Hoover Dam still controlling water flows, or had it crumbled away to flood everything in its path? Had the dams in Kenya gone back to being nothing more than sand? How much of the world would go from being covered by water to being covered by land and vice versa, just because mankind was no longer around to direct its flow? What would the world have looked like if man had never come along and learned about irrigation or hydroelectric power? Where would rivers have flowed over and created new rivers? Which parts of the world would be desert?

He spent the next evening in a city called Fredericton. Beautiful stone cathedrals could be seen in the distance, but both bridges connecting the two sides of the city were washed away, so he left without being able to get close to them.

He almost never saw what he considered to be real cities anymore. What he came across could barely even be considered towns. He passed places along the map that sounded as though they would be towns or cities—Washademoak, Dubee Settlement, Kinnear Settlement—

that turned out to be a collection of three or four houses followed by miles of fields.

On one stretch of road, he went thirty miles without seeing anywhere to sleep under cover. In these areas, there was no discernible difference between now and before the Great De-evolution. In some parts, the roads blended in with the forest; there were sections of road where he couldn't tell if he was still on the original path or in the brush next to what had been the road. In other parts, the passage had completely sunk into the marsh surrounding it. For what appeared to be a hundred yards, the road vanished and was replaced by green water so dirty that not even birds dared land near it. The swamp stretched on either side for as far as he could see. Parking lots were gone. Soccer fields were gone. There was no telling what nature would do next. Maybe a thousand years from now the entire section of earth would be a vast desert. Maybe it would be a series of lakes. Maybe something else.

It was getting dark by the time he approached Halifax. Immediately after the skyline came into view, he saw a puff of smoke rising in the air from the far corner of some outlying houses. He thought for a moment about turning around, but eventually continued toward the tiny stream of smoke and whoever lived there.

Chapter 16

An incredible amount of smoke was rising from the stadium. His senses deadened as he watched the sun get blotted out behind the black cloud. He saw the smoke, but not the birds flying away from it. He smelled the burning chemicals from miles away, but not the exhaust of the truck next to him on the road. He couldn't hear anything, not even the cars blaring their horns right next to him.

The man on the radio was saying something, but Jeffrey didn't hear this either. "There are thousands of people gathered around the stadium… The fire is getting out of control now. There were thousands of Blocks in that stadium."

Each time he tried calling Katherine, both at home and on her cell, it rang until her recorded voice picked up. All around him, cars were rear-ending each other or drifting into abandoned vehicles left in random places, all because everyone was staring at the spectacle in the distance rather than the road in front of them.

The other cars were also probably listening to the radio: "I don't know what's happening—the fire is everywhere now—oh my God—there's fire everywhere."

A driver was crying hysterically as she gazed at the fire. She took her hands off the steering wheel long enough to tear strips of hair off her scalp. Her car, only barely moving because of the traffic jam, angled slowly toward the metal guardrail.

Katherine's phone rang and rang, but there was no answer. As if in response to his calls, the man on the radio yelled, "Everything is on fire! The entire stadium is on fire! Everyone outside is leaving the area. The police are just walking away. The entire stadium is burning to the ground."

Blaring his horn did no good. None of the other drivers took their eyes off the dark cloud that was hypnotizing them.

The fire raged and raged.

Dear God, he thought, *please don't let my boy be in there*. But part of him, without having spoken to Katherine, without seeing his boy's burned flesh with his own two eyes, already knew that was Galen's fate. His lips didn't stop mumbling the prayer, but he knew everyone inside the stadium, his boy amongst them, would be dead.

Some of the cars were ramming each other in an attempt to get ahead faster. One car's bumper flew across two lanes into the guardrail, the driver oblivious to what was happening around him. Another car over-compensated after being side-swiped and veered off an embankment.

Why wouldn't Katherine answer her phone?

Some of the drivers were getting out of their cars because they could walk faster than the traffic. A man took three steps before the car behind him ran him over by accident. His crumpled body remained motionless on the highway as other cars passed by.

Jeffrey was surprised when Katherine answered her phone.

"Where are you?" he asked before she could say anything. "Are you at home?"

"No."

"Where are you?" he said again. "Tell me. Tell me you aren't near the stadium."

He was walking as he spoke. He passed a Mercedes with two flat tires, the old woman behind the wheel still trying to make her car move forward along the concrete.

Three helicopters were hovering above the stadium to get better footage of the fire.

Katherine was saying, "The guy on TV said everyone should bring their Blocks down to the stadium. He said they would help get all the Blocks down to Washington. He said—"

His phone fell to his side. A man ran past him, headed in the direction of the stadium. There was nothing left worth running to, but the man would need to learn that for himself.

When he brought the phone back to his ear, he asked, "Did you know what was going to happen?"

But Katherine was crying too much to answer. Finally, when she could speak, she started to say something about when they were younger—always with her, it was about the past. And that was when he tossed the phone away rather than hear an excuse for why their boy was dead.

He turned and started walking back to the base.

**

Past the city center, beyond a tiny bay lined with houses, the smoke's source came into view. The active fireplace belonged to a house located just before a giant wooded park. A man, roughly the same age as Jeffrey, was at the end of the driveway, an arm already waving hello as the tank approached. The man was by himself. Not even a dog by his side. Jeffrey climbed out and said hello.

"You must be really lost," the man said, smiling. "Where are you coming from?"

"I've been traveling up the east coast. But I'm originally from Philadelphia."

"Awful thing that happened there," the man said. But before Jeffrey could offer a response, the man had turned back toward his house. "I was just about to fix some coffee. You want some?"

As they drank, the man said his name was Art and asked Jeffrey what his name was. But in between every question, Jeffrey kept looking out the windows for somebody to sneak up to his tank and steal it.

"Trust me," Art said, "it's just me and the animals. There hasn't been another person through these parts in a very long time. Nova Scotia wasn't exactly a popular place to visit once everyone was trying to get down to New England, or even further south."

"Why did you stay?"

"I'm still not sure," the man said. "The only answer I can come up with is that it has something to do with being stubborn and dumb. I'd like to have a better reason, but I think it boils down to that. I was thirty when my sister, her husband, and my parents all decided to head south. As soon as they said I had to go with them, my dumbass decided I had to stay. I had a lot of reasons why I thought I had to stay, but looking back, none of them really mattered, and all of them must have sounded painfully naïve when my parents and sister listened to me. They only left without me when I convinced them I would eventually head down too. I still have no idea why I felt like I had to make the trip by myself instead of with them."

Jeffrey thought back to all the dumb things he had said and done when he was younger. It still surprised him that Katherine had put up with him in high school and college, back when he had been at his most immature and selfish. Half the things he had done in his life had only been carried out because someone else told him not to do them. No better reason.

"Did your family go to Boston or New York?" Jeffrey asked.

Art shook his head. "The folks around here took their boats. My parents and my sister went straight down to Florida on their thirty-footer. I was going to do the same thing, but of course that was when Hurricane Tori wiped us out. There wasn't a single sea-faring ship in these parts after that storm. It gave me a lot of time to wonder why I'd been so adamant about staying here by myself."

Jeffrey looked in the direction of the water. "This part of the world is beautiful."

"That it is," Art said. "That it is. I've been here all my life and I still smile every time I step outside because of the hills and the trees. We went on a field trip to New York—the city—when I was a little kid. It was really neat for the first couple of hours, but even as a kid I got tired of it pretty fast. I imagine every other city to be the same way. But then again, I wouldn't really know."

"You'd be surprised," Jeffrey said. "Places blend together. Especially these days."

They didn't say anything for a while. The longer Jeffrey looked out the window the more cats and dogs he saw wandering the streets and the forest.

Art followed Jeffrey's eyes. "I used to take care of them. I had five pets at first. Then ten. Then twenty. After a while I lost count. Then I realized I was just encouraging them to stay around my house instead of going off on their own. If you ever go over to Big Indian Lake, you'll be amazed. The entire area has turned into a cat sanctuary. There are thousands of them there. They're nice mostly, but a couple of them are starting to get too wild. They eye you up like you're the next meal. Poor little things don't know how to take care of themselves either. I find hundreds of them over there each spring that have either frozen to death or starved to death. I tried to set a giant bonfire for them one year, so they would have a source of heat during the coldest months. Stupid me, I almost burned down the entire forest."

Art asked if Jeffrey would like to stay for lunch, but he shook his head and said he didn't want to overstay his welcome.

"You're the first person I've seen in more than a decade," the man said. "You could piss on my kitchen floor and you wouldn't be overstaying your welcome."

On his way back out the front door, Jeffrey paused and said, "I've been traveling a lot. Do you mind if I stay in a house down the road?"

Art laughed. "Do I mind if you stay in a house down the road? You can stay anywhere you want."

That night, as he was walking around from empty room to empty room in his new house, Jeffrey found himself thinking about the people who used to call this very place their home. A husband and wife would be in one room. Their sons and daughters in other places throughout the house. Each room sat empty now. He spent the night there, but in the morning he packed what few things he had and explored the area.

He walked to Art's house again the following day.

"Welcome, neighbor," Art said with a smile. "You like Atlantic whitefish?"

Jeffrey noticed there were too many fish on the grill for one person. There was even a second plate ready to be served with food.

"Of course I do. Who doesn't?" Jeffrey said, even though he didn't know that kind of fish from any other.

While they ate, Jeffrey asked if Art still kept in touch with his family. He had no idea why he was asking; it wasn't his business and it wasn't his nature to pry into others' business.

Tiny flakes of fish fell out of the man's mouth when he spoke. "My mother passed away three years ago. But I still talk to my father every week. And of course I'm always talking to my sis."

And then it was only natural that Art ask about Jeffery's family. He could have lied and said he didn't have any family at all; that would kill the conversation or get it onto something else.

But instead, he said, "I write to my mom and dad every once in a while. They're down in Florida too."

"That's good," Art said.

"Would you mind if I settled down around these parts?"

The man chuckled again. "You ask some really funny questions. Do whatever you want."

A couple of days later Jeffrey decided to go north to see the rest of Nova Scotia. It was getting cold again so he packed an extra blanket and sweater. He still took peanut butter and jelly sandwiches with him whenever he went out for the day. As he left, he wondered if Art would think he was leaving for good and if it mattered either way.

It took Jeffrey a day to get back to the town of Truro. It took another day to get to the bridge that connected the main portion of Nova Scotia with the northern quarter of land. The bridge was gone. He found a working radio, but there was nothing except uninterrupted static from one end of the dial to the other. An entire section of land, as big as New Jersey, was out of man's grasp again.

Maybe in ten more years, everything north of the Mississippi river would be cut off from the people in the final settlements, until, one day, even the bridges in and around Miami and Los Angeles would begin to deteriorate and the people there would be stuck in the final two decaying cities.

He still thought about the times he and Galen and Katherine had gone to the beach together. As his eyes closed one night, he thought of the greatest gift Galen had given him: Jeffrey had never felt pressure to impress his son or to live up to the expectations that only a child could create for their parents.

He remembered a time when he had been in first grade and all of the other boys' moms or dads went to school to talk to the class about their jobs, but Jeffrey's father had been in New York on business and couldn't be there. And even if he could have been there, he remembered being nervous that his father's job as a textile supervisor would embarrass him in front of the other kids. All his father cared about was providing for his family and yet there Jeffrey was, a typical, unappreciative kid, not concerned with the long hours his father worked or all the dreams he had given up on in order to provide for his wife and child.

Galen had never made him feel that pressure, that unsubstantiated embarrassment. He had never felt fear over whether or not his son might be ashamed of what he did. He could have been a garbage man or a brain surgeon and his son would still sit on the porch with him each evening. That in itself was enough to have loved the boy.

Soon after returning to Halifax, he went to Art's house. With him, he carried a big plate of pancakes. The other man's face brightened at the offering.

"How was your vacation?" Art said as they stood by his food processor to make a batch of fake syrup.

"I tried to go see the Highlands National Park but the bridge was out."

"I could have told you that. That bridge was out before my family sailed south. You could have taken my Kayak across the water if you were really interested."

Jeffrey imagined himself in a tiny boat with an oar in his hands. "I didn't want to see it that badly." After another bite of pancakes, he asked, "Do you ever think about going down and joining your family?"

"Of course. I think about it all the time. But not even I'm stubborn enough to think I can make it south in a kayak. That would be suicide." He shoveled another bite of pancakes into his mouth.

"Does Halifax have a nice library?" Jeffrey asked.

Again, Art chuckled. "Always with the odd questions. Yes, it has a very nice library."

They didn't say anything else until both plates were clear of food. When Jeffrey did speak, he said, "If you'd like my tank, you can take it to go down to Florida."

"I don't know the first thing about driving a tank."

"Believe it or not, neither did I until I took this one."

"You don't need it?"

"I think I'm done with it. I've gone as far as I can go."

The man looked out the window and smiled. "A random guy shows up here after everyone else has been gone for years, then offers me a tank. This is an amazing world."

He accepted the offer right away. The only thing left was to learn how to maneuver the tank so it got him where he wanted to go. And for the first time since coming into possession of the tank, Jeffrey had somebody in the cockpit with him. He went over what each lever did, explained what the tank could do and what it couldn't do, then gave a list of bridges he knew of that had collapsed. And when the explanations were over, Jeffrey climbed back out, handed Art's bags down to him, and watched the hatch shut.

From within the tank he heard Art's voice. "I still can't believe this is happening. Thank you so much."

And then the tank's engine came to life. A moment later the machine started in the direction Jeffrey had originally come from. The tank could still be heard after it had disappeared from sight. When the noise faded away, Jeffrey walked down to the water.

The cold Canadian water signaled the approach of yet another winter. As he watched the tiny waves lap against the rocks, he got the feeling that he needed to call home. Not to his parents, but what had been *his* home. The phone rang and rang. He expected it to either keep ringing forever, or for an operator's recorded voice to tell him the number was no longer in service, but eventually Katherine's old message came on and said that neither she, nor Jeffrey, nor Galen could come to the phone, and to please leave a message.

Beep.

"Hi, it's me. I don't know if you're still there or not. I guess it doesn't really matter one way or the other. I just wanted to say that I forgive you. I'll never agree with what you did, but I forgive you. That's all."

That night, as he sat on a wooden bench, watching the sun go down behind the trees, the ocean side already dark, he found himself thinking about how incredible it was to be near the water in that moment, to see the immensity of the ocean rubbing against the stones, listening to the water's constant, soothing noises. And he thought about how nice it had been to be able to share similar moments with Galen years earlier.

Instead of wishing his son was still with him right then, however, he remembered those past memories with fondness as he thought about the new memories he had yet to make. His boy had moved on. He would move on one day as well. All things would. That was part of the lesson the Great De-evolution was trying to teach.

With the final moments of light left in the evening, the sight of water faded to only its sounds. And then those too ebbed away, and there was only silence. And he added that moment to the set of new memories he started to build, being thankful for what he had instead of missing that which he didn't.

A day would come, maybe not for another decade, maybe not for three, when he would take his final breaths. And maybe he would see his son again then. Maybe he wouldn't. And a day would come when the very last man or woman would take their last breath too, and the world would return to a simpler time. Some things were certain and some things could never be known.

But as the sun set over the hill, as the sky became

black and the waves vanished from sight, he didn't concern himself with any of that. He would wake up the next day and the waves would be there.

That would be enough.

ACKNOLWEDGEMENTS

I am once again indebted to many people for their support: as always, Jodie McFadden, for her constant encouragement and optimism; Derek Prior, for a great edit of the manuscript; and everyone at Authors On The Air, GoodReads, and in the BJJ and MMA communities who read my other novels and recommended them to their friends. Without their support, I would be no where.

ABOUT THE AUTHOR

Chris graduated from Western Maryland College (McDaniel College). His dream is to write the same kind of stories that have inspired him over the years.

His others novels have become Amazon Best Sellers, been featured on Authors on the Air, and were voted as some of GoodReads top 10 "Most Interesting Books" the year they were published.

Manufactured by Amazon.ca
Bolton, ON

29386661R00148